THE BEST OF
MARY DIANA DODS

THE BEST OF
MARY DIANA DODS

AN AUTHOR AHEAD OF THEIR TIME

WALTER SHOLTO DOUGLAS   MARY DIANA DODS
DAVID LYNDSAY

Foreword by
NATASHA TIDD
Edited by
ANNA STILESKI

WFP
WORDFIRE PRESS

The Best of Mary Diana Dods: An Author Ahead of Their Time contains the following works:

THE PREDICTION by MARY DIANA DODS, originally published in Tales of the Wild and the Wonderful, 1927.

DER FREISCHÜTZ; OR, THE MAGIC BALLS by MARY DIANA DODS, originally published in Tales of the Wild and the Wonderful, 1927.

THE LORD OF THE MAELSTROM by MARY DIANA DODS, originally published in Tales of the Wild and the Wonderful, 1927.

THE RING AND THE STREAM by DAVID LYNDSAY, originally published in Blackwood's Edinburgh Magazine, 1822.

These works are in the public domain.

This new edition edited by Anna Stileski

Foreword copyright © 2022 by Natasha Tidd

EBook ISBN: 978-1-68057-360-2
Trade Paperback ISBN: 978-1-68057-359-6
Hardcover ISBN: 978-1-68057-361-9
Cover design by Justin Scott
Cover artwork image by Justin Scott

Published by WordFire Press, LLC
PO Box 1840
Monument CO 80132
Kevin J. Anderson & Rebecca Moesta, Publishers
WordFire Press Edition 2022
Printed in the USA
Join our WordFire Press Readers Group for new projects, and giveaways. Sign up at wordfirepress.com

CONTENTS

FOREWORD

NATASHA TIDD

This book marks the first time in over 200 years that David Lyndsay's 1825 book, *Tales of the Wild and the Wonderful*, and their acclaimed work for *Blackwood's Magazine* will be published in one compendium under their birth name, Mary Diana Dods. However, in any publishing of Dods's work it would be remiss to not include the third name that Dods went under: Walter Sholto Douglas. Although Dods was born as Mary Diana Dods sometime around 1790, they lived the latter part of their life as Walter Sholto Douglas, a name they would die under sometime in late 1829 or early 1830 in a Parisian debtor's prison.

Although Dods's close friends, such as Mary Shelley, knew both of the Lyndsay pen name and transition to Sholto Douglas, Dods's three identities were lost to history until the 1980s. Prior to this, historians had assumed that Dods, Lyndsay and Sholto Douglas were separate people, basing this on individual letters sent to Mary Shelley, as well as David Lyndsay's work and letters with *Blackwood's* magazine (Dods's editors didn't know Lyndsay was a pseudonym). In 1980, historian and Mary Shelley expert, Betty T Bennett, noticed similarities between the Dods, Lyndsay and Sholto Douglas letters. This began a decade-long investigation by Bennett, who was the first to discover that the mysterious trio were, in fact, one person. Bennett published this research in her 1991 book, *Mary Diana Dods, a Gentleman and a Scholar*.

Bennett hypothesised that Dods moved to Paris to start a new life as a foreign diplomat, which she cites as the reason why the last known published piece of writing of Lyndsay is from an 1828 compendium of fiction, *The Pledge of Friendship for 1828*. As a woman, Dods would not have been able to secure diplomatic work, so Bennett suggests that Dods 'cross-dressed,' assuming the name, Walter Sholto Douglas. Bennet attributes Sholto Douglas's death in a male debtor's prison as a sign that *'Dods had all but lost her mind'* due to the elaborate scheme she'd created. Today, Bennett's findings offer the most well-known iteration of Mary Diana Dods life. However, in the thirty years since Bennett completed her research, the field of Transgender Studies has made great strides, increasing our understanding within psychology, sexology, anthropology and history. This has led several historians, including myself, to reanalyse the evidence we have on Dods, Lyndsay and Sholto Douglas. It seems very likely that Walter Sholto Douglas was a trans man. The ploy to start a life as a diplomat has scant evidential support, only found fleetingly mentioned once (in a late 1827 letter to Mary Shelley from mutual friend, Harriett Garnett). Additionally, Sholto Douglas seemingly made no attempt to work as a diplomat. The move to Paris was in fact probably a chance for Sholto Douglas to start a new life as a man in a country where nobody knew them as Mary Diana Dods.

There are several indications that prior to the 1827 move, Mary Diana Dods was known to be, at least in some ways, masculine presenting. In the second part of her 1860 autobiography, socialite Eliza Rennie recalled meeting Dods at a party; *'Nature in any of its wild vagaries never fashioned anything more grotesque looking than was this, Miss Dods... you almost fancied, on first looking at her, that someone of the masculine gender had indulged in the masquerade freak of feminine habiliments and that 'Miss Dods was an alias for Mr.'* Bar Rennie's musings, not much is written of Dods within literary society. They are known only as a quiet but intelligent wallflower who is a friend of Mary Shelley. That friendship seems to have been crucial for Dods, for Shelley was not only a close friend, but an ally; the pair bonding over their writing, reading each other's work and pushing one another to improve. Soon Shelley became one of the few people to know of the Lyndsay pen name. And it's in Shelley's letters from Dods (who she affectionately calls 'D' or 'Doddy') that it becomes apparent that society's view of Dods as a shy intellectual couldn't be further from the truth. This writer is an erudite, slightly flirtatious and deeply passionate person with a wicked sense of humour and no-nonsense attitude. Their letters are as exhausting and exhilarating as their fiction is.

Lyndsay's first known published work, *The Plague of Darkness*, appeared in the August 1821 edition of *Blackwood's Magazine*, and their first book, *Dreams of The Ancient World*, was published that same year. David Lyndsay primarily published in *Blackwood's Magazine*, a literary paper that was known for work by some of the day's best writers. The owner, William Blackwood, was deeply impressed by Lyndsay's prose and, after *The Plague of Darkness* was published, he eagerly wrote to friends and colleagues of his desire to meet the enigmatic young writer. By 1823, Lyndsay was still regularly contributing, but had also expanded to other publications, their work included in the likes of *The Literary Pocket Book*, alongside John Keats and a posthumous poem of Percy Bysshe Shelley. Lyndsay was becoming well known as a writer, so it's perhaps surprising that in 1826, just months after the 1825 publishing of *Tales of the Wild and the Wonderful*, Dods dropped the Lyndsay pen name, instead taking up the pseudonym Douglas Sholto.

Only two pieces of Dods's work are known to have been

published in 1826, both back-to-back in the July and August editions of *Blackwood's* and both under Douglas Sholto; *The Owl* and *My Transmogrifications*. This literary detour only lasted a year, with David Lyndsay once more appearing in 1827, with the publication *of The Bridal Ornaments: A legend of Thuringia*. However, Dods's time writing under Douglas Sholto is notable not just for the work created, but for its timing. Its publication seems to have coincided with a key event in their life. During that July and August, *Blackwood's* received a series of letters from a woman named Isabella Sholto, who identified herself as the wife of Douglas Sholto. Isabella was not another pen name, but Isabella Robinson, a young London socialite and mutual friend of both Shelley and Dods. The next time we see Dods is in September 1827, following the July death of their father, George Douglas, 16th Earl of Morton. We learn from Shelley's letters that throughout July and August Robinson had been staying with her, whilst awaiting the return of her husband who was in Scotland attending their father's funeral. Upon Isabella's husband's return, Shelley wrote that the pair were planning to move to France. Finally, in late September, 'D' and Isabella reunited and we learn that Dods is indeed Isabella's husband (not legally but publicly), now goes by Walter Sholto Douglas, and is living openly as a man. Upon their arrival, work immediately begins on the couple's international move. In late September 1827, Shelley and the actor John Howard Payne helped Sholto Douglas illegally acquire fake documentation with this new name, which could then be used to forge a life in France. The final pieces in place, Walter and Isabella left England, settling in Paris in November 1827. Almost immediately they are welcomed into Parisian society, Garnett becoming one of the first to write of the pair, noting Isabella for her charms and Walter as a warm and intellectual husband.

Society functions aside, it seems that Walter Sholto Douglas continued writing as David Lyndsay whilst in Paris. Lyndsay's work was regularly published throughout 1827, primarily by *Blackwood's*, and Shelley helped her friend by sending their work to editors alongside her own in both 1827 and 1828. The reason for Lyndsay's sudden literary disappearance in 1828 appears to be due to ill health. We know from the Eliza Rennie that Dods suffered from chronic pain and *'the existence of some organic disease'* that physically affected them. In the last days of 1827, Garnett notes that Sholto Douglas's health appears to be in rapid decline and as 1828 progresses, they are seen publicly less and less. Then in a letter dated 28-29th June, Mary Shelley writes of Sholto Douglas; *'What D. now is, I will not describe in a letter, one only trusts that the diseased body acts on the diseased and that both mind and body will be at rest ere long.'* As their health failed, so did the Douglas marriage. Isabella embarked on a very public affair with the philosopher, Claude Charles Fauriel. The couple were also racking up debt, with Walter unable to work and write, Isabella steadfast on maintaining their role in society. It is at this point Walter Sholto Douglas once more drops out of our historic lens, their health failing, their writing career stalled, and drowning in debt. They then appear a year later in November 1829 in a letter to Isabella's former lover Fauriel from his new flame, Mary Clarke, who reports that Sholto Douglas has been sent to debtors' prison. Clarke requested a friend, one Mr Fisher, to bring them a fake moustache and whiskers. This throwaway anecdote is the last we hear of Dods, Lyndsay or Sholto Douglas. The trail then runs cold, with them alone in a debtor's prison far from home, where they died sometime in late 1829 or early 1830.

Although this book is published under their birth name, the life of Walter Sholto Douglas is just as an important factor in the works you are about to read. As will become transparent in the foreword 'Lyndsay' wrote to *Tales of the Wild and the Wonderful*, their work was deeply personal and a reflection of who they were as a person and what they experienced. Above all it is the work of an exhausting but brilliant mind, whose career was cut too short.

—Natasha Tidd
London, UK
1 March 2022

AUTHOR'S NOTE

TO THE READER.

Pause one moment, gentle Reader—only one little moment will I detain you, while I reply to the question which I have supposed you to ask in the title page. Blame not me, I beseech you, if you are compelled to make the usual accusation against authors, that there is nothing new in the pages which I diffidently present to you: I am sorry for it, but I cannot help it. Solomon asserted that all things under the sun were aged in his time; and if the wisest of old gentlemen could find nothing new in that early stage of his empire, what can be expected from a poor scribbler like me, near three thousand years after him? Consider too, dear Reader, that this is the first time I have appeared before you in the character of a storyteller; and that I am a timid, nervous subject, and very easily discouraged. Accept me then upon the score of wishing to amuse you, and permit me to say something for my Tales, after having said so much for myself.

Of the stories, "Der Freischütz," as everybody knows, is from the German. "The Fortunes of De la Pole" is original; so is "The Prediction," and "The Yellow Dwarf," if I may be allowed that claim for such a "thing of shreds and patches;" it is an *olla podrida* of odds and ends, a snip of the garment of every fairy tale written since the days of King Arthur. The last story, "The Lord of the Maelstrom," is also original, though, as in that of "The Yellow Dwarf," I have raised my structure upon an old nursery foundation; but it appeared to me an excellent vehicle for the beautiful mythology of the North, and the introduction of Odin and his exploits—whose history, by the way, I believe, has been extracted from the Talmud, or from the rabbinical traditions of the events previous to the creation, and the deeds of Moses and others. I, moreover, designed to have given thee a little poetry for thy money, gentle Reader, but the booksellers shook their heads when I mentioned my design, and told me it was out of fashion; so I returned my treasures in that way to my desk, there to remain, among many other excellent things, I assure thee, until it should again be the taste in England; and, in the meantime, offer these Tales of *diablerie* for your amusement. Entreat me kindly, gentle Reader, I beseech you, for two reasons; first, because it will entirely depend, upon your reception of this, whether I shall ever write a second volume—and secondly, because there has been a sad sweep lately among those who used to cater for your diversion: many who were most deserving have been snatched from your admiration and regard. "Shelley is not—Lord Byron is not—and Maturin have they taken away." For myself, I am not a long-lived man, and therefore advise you to make much of me while I am with you; and as an example, look upon these *"coglionerie"* with a milder eye than their merits may seem to deserve from your judgment.

I am, dear Reader, truly yours,
THE AUTHOR.

THE PREDICTION

THE PREDICTION

"Let's talk of Graves."
SHAKESPEARE

On the southwest coast of the principality of Wales stands a romantic little village, inhabited chiefly by the poorer class of people, consisting of small farmers and oyster dredgers, whose estates are the wide ocean, and whose ploughs are the small craft in which they glide over its interminable fields in search of the treasures which they wring from its bosom; it is built on the very top of a hill, commanding on the one side, a view of an immense bay, and on the other, of the peaceful green fields and valleys, cultivated by the greater number of its quiet inhabitants. The approach to it from the nearest town was by a road which branched away into lanes and wooded walks, and from the sea by a beautiful little bay, running up far into the land; both sides of which, and indeed all the rest of the coast, were guarded by craggy and gigantic rocks, some of them hollowed into caverns, into which none of the inhabitants, from motives of superstition, reverence, and fear, had ever dared to penetrate.

There were, at the period of which we are about to treat, no better sort of inhabitants in the little village just described, none of those so emphatically distinguished as "quality" by the country people; they had neither parson, lawyer, nor doctor, among them, and of course there was a tolerable equality among the residents. The farmer, who followed his own plough in the spring, singing the sweet wild national chaunt of the season, and bound up with his own hands his sheaves in the autumn, was not richer, greater, nor finer, than he who, bare-legged on the strand, gathered in the hoar weed for the farmer in the spring, or dared the wild winds of autumn and the wrath of the winter in his little boat, to earn with his dredging net a yet harder subsistence for his family. Distinctions were unknown in the village, every man was the equal of his neighbour.

But, though rank and its polished distinctions were strange in the village of N—, the superiority of talent was felt and acknowledged almost without a pause or a murmur. There was one who was as a king amongst them, by the mere force of a mightier spirit than those with whom he sojourned had been accustomed to feel among them: he was a dark and moody man, a stranger, evidently of a higher order than those around him, who had but a few months before, without any apparent object, settled among them: he was poor, but had no occupation—he lived frugally, but quite alone—and his sole employments were to read during the day, and wander out unaccompanied into the fields or by the beach during the night. Sometimes indeed he would relieve a suffering child or rheumatic old man by medicinal herbs, reprove idleness and drunkenness in the youth, and predict to all the good and evil consequences of their conduct; and his success in some cases, his foresight in others, and his wisdom in all, won for him a high reputation among the cottagers, to which his taciturn habits contributed not a little, for, with the vulgar as with the educated, no talker was ever seriously taken for a conjuror, though a silent man is often decided to be a wise one.

There was but one person in N— at all disposed to rebel against the despotic sovereignty which Rhys Meredith was silently establishing over the quiet village, and that was precisely the person most likely to effect a revolution; she was a beautiful maiden, the glory and boast of the village, who had been the favourite of, and to a certain degree educated by, the late lady of the lord of the manor; but she had died, and her pupil, with a full consciousness of her intellectual superiority, had returned to her native village, where she determined to have an empire of her own, which no rival should dispute: she laughed at the maidens who listened to the predictions of Rhys, and she refused her smiles to the youths who consulted him upon their affairs and their prospects; and as the beautiful Ruth was generally beloved, the silent Rhys was soon in danger of being abandoned by all, save doting men and paralytic women, and feeling himself an outcast in the village of N—.

But to be such was not the object of Meredith; he was an idle man, and the gifts of the villagers contributed to spare him from exertion; he knew too, that in another point of view this ascendancy was necessary to his purposes; and as he had failed to establish it by wisdom and benevolence, he determined to try the effect of fear. The character of the people with whom he sojourned was admirably calculated to assist his projects; his predictions were now uttered more clearly, and his threats denounced in sterner tones and stronger and plainer words; and when he predicted that old Morgan Williams, who had been stricken with the palsy, would die at the turn of tide, three days from that on which he spoke, and that the light little boat of gay Griffy Morris, which sailed from the bay in a bright winter's morning, should never again make the shore; and the man died, and the storm arose, even as he had said; men's hearts died within them, and they bowed down before his words, as if he had been their general fate and the individual destiny of each.

Ruth's rosy lip grew pale for a moment as she heard of these things; in the next her spirit returned, and "I will make him tell my fortune," she said, as she went with a party of laughers to search out and deride the conjuror. He was alone when they broke in upon him, and their mockeries goaded his spirit; but his anger was deep, not loud; and while burning with wrath, he yet could calmly consider the means of vengeance: he knew the master spirit with which he had to contend; it was no ordinary mind, and would have smiled at ordinary terrors. To have threatened her with sickness, misfortune, or death, would have been to call forth the energies of that lofty spirit, and prepare it to endure, and it would have gloried in manifesting its powers of endurance; he must humble it therefore by debasement; he must ruin its confidence in itself; and to this end he resolved to threaten her with crime. His resolution was taken and effected; his credit was at stake; he must daunt his enemy, or surrender to her power: he foretold sorrows and joys to the listening throng, not according to his passion, but his judgment, and he drew a blush upon the cheek of one, by revealing a secret which Ruth herself, and another, alone knew, and which prepared the former to doubt of her own judgment, as it related to this extraordinary man.

Ruth was the last who approached to hear the secret of her destiny. The wizard paused as he looked upon her—opened his book, shut it, paused, and again looked sadly and fearfully upon her; she tried to smile, but felt startled, she knew not why; the bright inquiring glance of her dark eye could not change the purpose of her enemy.

Her smile could not melt, nor even temper, the hardness of his deep-seated malice: he again looked sternly upon her brow, and then coldly wrung out the slow soul-withering words, "Maiden, thou art doomed to be a murderer!"

From that hour Rhys Meredith became the destiny of Ruth Tudor. At first she spurned at his prediction, and alternately cursed and laughed at him for the malice of his falsehood: but when she found that none laughed with her, that men looked upon her with suspicious eyes, women shrunk from her society, and children shrieked at her presence, she felt that these were signs of truth, and her high spirit no longer struggled against the conviction; a change came over her mind when she had known how horrid it was to be alone. Abhorring the prophet, she yet clung to his footsteps, and while she sat by his side, felt as if he alone could avert that evil destiny which he alone had foreseen. With him only was she seen to smile; elsewhere, sad, silent, stern; it seemed as if she were ever occupied in nerving her mind for that which she had to do, and her beauty, already of the majestic cast, grew absolutely awful, as her perfect features assumed an expression which might have belonged to the angel of vengeance or death.

But there were moments when her naturally strong spirit, not yet wholly subdued, struggled against her conviction, and endeavoured to find modes of averting her fate: it was in one of these, perhaps, that she gave her hand to a wooer, from a distant part of the country, a sailor, who either had not heard, or did not regard the prediction of Rhys, upon condition that he should remove her far from her native village to the home of his family and friends, for she sometimes felt as if the decree which had gone forth against her could not be fulfilled except upon the spot where she had heard it, and that her heart would be lighter if men's eyes would again look upon her in kindliness, and she no longer sate beneath the glare of those that knew so well the secret of her soul. Thus thinking, she quitted N— with her husband; and the tormentor, who had poisoned her repose, soon after her departure, left the village as secretly and as suddenly as he had entered it.

But, though Ruth could depart from his corporeal presence,

and look upon his cruel visage no more, yet the eye of her soul was fixed upon his shadow, and his airy form, the creation of her sorrow, still sat by her side; the blight that he had breathed upon her peace had withered her heart, and it was in vain that she sought to forget or banish the recollection from her brain. Men and women smiled upon her as before in the days of her joy, the friends of her husband welcomed her to their bosoms, but they could give no peace to her heart: she shrunk from their friendship, she shivered equally at their neglect, she dreaded any cause that might lead to that which, it had been said, she must do; nightly she sat alone and thought, she dwelt upon the characters of those around her, and shuddered that in some she saw violence and selfishness enough to cause injury, which she might be supposed to resent to blood. Then she wept bitter tears and thought of her native village, whose inhabitants were so mild, and whose previous knowledge of her hapless destiny might induce them to avoid all that might hasten its completion, and sighed to think she had ever left it in the mistaken hope of finding peace elsewhere. Again, her sick fancy would ponder upon the modes of murder, and wonder how her victim would fall. Against the use of actual violence she had disabled herself; she had never struck a blow, her small hand would have suffered injury in the attempt; she understood not the usage of fire-arms, she was ignorant of what were poisons, and a knife she never allowed herself, even for the most necessary purposes: how then could she slay?

At times she took comfort from thoughts like these, and at others, in the blackness of her despair, she would cry, "If it must be, O let it come, and these miserable anticipations cease; then I shall, at least, destroy but one; now, in my incertitude, I am the murderer of many!"

Her husband went forth and returned upon the voyages which made up the avocation and felicity of his life, without noticing the deep-rooted sorrow of his wife; he was a common man, and of a common mind; his eye had not seen the awful beauty of her whom he had chosen; his spirit had not felt her power; and, if he had marked, he would not have understood her grief; so she ministered to him as a duty. She was a silent and obedient wife, but she saw him come home without joy, and witnessed his departure without regret; he neither added to nor diminished her sorrow: but destiny had one solitary blessing in store for the victim of its decrees, a child was born to the hapless Ruth, a lovely little girl soon slept upon her bosom, and, coming as it did, the one lone and lovely rose-bud in her desolate garden, she welcomed it with a warmer joy and cherished it with a kindlier hope.

A few years went by unsoiled by the wretchedness which had marked the preceding; the joy of the mother softened the anguish of the condemned, and sometimes when she looked upon her daughter she ceased to despair: but destiny had not forgotten her claim, and soon her hand pressed heavily upon her victim; the giant ocean rolled over the body of her husband, poverty visited the cottage of the widow, and famine's gaunt figure was visible in the distance. Oppression came with these, for arrears of rent were demanded, and he who asked was brutal in his anger and harsh in his language to the sufferers. Ruth shuddered as she heard him speak, and trembled for him and for herself; the unforgotten prophecy arose in her mind, and she preferred even witnesses to his brutality and her degradation, rather than encounter his anger and her own dark thoughts alone.

Thus goaded, she saw but one thing that could save her, she fled from her persecutors to the home of her youth, and, leading her little Rachel by the hand, threw herself into the arms of her kin: they received her with distant kindness, and assured her that she should not want: in this they kept their promise, but it was all they did for Ruth and her daughter; a miserable subsistence was given to them, and that was embittered by distrust, and the knowledge that it was yielded unwillingly.

Among the villagers, although she was no longer shunned as formerly, her story was not forgotten; if it had been, her terrific beauty, the awful flashing of her eyes, her large black curls hanging like thunderclouds over her stern and stately brow and marble throat, her majestic stature, and solemn movements, would have recalled it to their recollections. She was a marked being, and all believed (though each would have pitied her, had they not been afraid) that her evil destiny was not to be averted; she looked like one fated to some wonderful deed. They saw she was not of them, and though they did not directly avoid her, yet they never threw themselves in her way, and thus the hapless Ruth had ample leisure to contemplate and grieve over her fate.

One night she sat alone in her wretched hovel, and, with many bitter ruminations, was watching the happy sleep of her child, who slumbered tranquilly on their only bed: midnight had long passed, yet Ruth was not disposed to rest; she trimmed her dull light, and said mentally, "Were I not poor, such a temptation might not assail me, riches would procure me deference; but poverty, or the wrongs it brings, may drive me to this evil; were I above want it would be less likely to be. O, my child, for thy sake would I avoid this doom more than for mine own, for if it should bring death to me, what will it not hurl on thee?— infamy, agony, scorn."

She wept aloud as she spoke, and scarcely seemed to notice the singularity (at that late hour) of someone without, attempting to open the door; she heard, but the circumstance made little impression; she knew that as yet her doom was unfulfilled, and that, therefore, no danger could reach her; she was no coward at any time, but now despair had made her brave; the door opened and a stranger entered, without either alarming or disturbing her, and it was not till he had stood face to face with Ruth, and discovered his features to be those of

Rhys Meredith, that she sprung up from her seat and gazed wildly and earnestly upon him.

Meredith gave her no time to question; "Ruth Tudor," said he, "behold the cruelest of thy foes comes suing to thy pity and mercy; I have embittered thy existence, and doomed thee to a terrible lot; what first was dictated by vengeance and malice became truth as I uttered it, for what I spoke I believed. Yet, take comfort, some of my predictions have failed, and why may not this be false? In my own fate I have ever been deceived, perhaps I may be equally so in thine; in the meantime have pity upon him who was thy enemy, but who, when his vengeance was uttered, instantly became thy friend. I was poor, and thy scorn might have robbed me of subsistence in danger, and thy contempt might have given me up. Beggared by many disastrous events, hunted by creditors, I fled from my wife and son because I could no longer bear to contemplate their suffering; I sought fortune all ways since we parted, and always has she eluded my grasp till last night, when she rather tempted than smiled upon me. At an idle fair I met the steward of this estate drunk and stupid, but loaded with gold; he travelled towards home alone; I could not, did not wrestle with the fiend that possessed me, but hastened to overtake him in his lonely ride.—Start not! no hair of his head was harmed by me; of his gold I robbed him, but not of his life, though, had I been the greater villain, I should now be in less danger, since he saw and marked my person: three hundred pounds is the meed of my daring, and I must keep it now or die. Ruth, thou too art poor and forsaken, but thou art faithful and kind, and wilt not betray me to justice; save me, and I will not enjoy my riches alone; thou knowest all the caves in the rocks, those hideous hiding places, where no foot, save thine, has dared to tread; conceal me in these till the pursuit be past, and I will give thee one half my wealth, and return with the other to gladden my wife and son."

The hand of Ruth was already opened, and in imagination

she grasped the wealth he promised; oppression and poverty had somewhat clouded the nobleness, but not the fierceness of her spirit. She saw that riches would save her from wrath, perhaps from blood, and, as the means to escape so mighty an evil, she was not scrupulous respecting a lesser: independently of this, she felt a great interest in the safety of Rhys; her own fate seemed to hang upon his; she hid the ruffian in the caves and supplied him with light and food.

There was a happiness now in the heart of Ruth—a joy in her thoughts as she sat all the long day upon the deserted settle of her wretched fire-side, to which they had for many years been strangers. Many times during the past years of her sorrow she hath thought of Rhys, and longed to look upon his face and sit beneath his shadow, as one whose presence could preserve her from the evil fate which he himself had predicted. She had long since forgiven him his prophecy; she believed he had spoken truth, and this gave her a wild confidence in his power; a confidence that sometimes thought, "if he can foreknow, can he not also avert?" She said mentally, without any reference to the temporal good he had promised her, "I have a treasure in those caves; *he* is there; he who hath foreseen and may oppose my destiny; he hath shadowed my days with sorrow, and forbidden me, like ordinary beings, to hope: yet he is now in my power; his life is in my hands; he says so, yet I believe him not, for I cannot betray him if I would; were I to lead the officers of justice to the spot where he lies crouching, he would be invisible to their sight or to mine; or I should become speechless ere I could say, 'Behold him.' No, he cannot die by me!"

And she thought she would deserve his confidence, and support him in his suffering; she had concealed him in a deep dark cave, hewn far in the rock, to which she alone knew the entrance from the beach; there was another (if a huge aperture in the top of the rock might be so called), which, far from attempting to descend, the peasants and seekers for the culprit had scarcely dared to look into, so perpendicular, dark, and uncertain was the hideous descent into what justly appeared to them a bottomless abyss; they passed over his head in their search through the fields above, and before the mouth of his den upon the beach below, yet they left him in safety, though in incertitude and fear.

It was less wonderful, the suspicionless conduct of the villagers towards Ruth, than the calm prudence with which she conducted all the details relating to her secret; her poverty was well known, yet she daily procured a double portion of food, which was won by double labour; she toiled in the fields for the meed of oaten cake and potatoes, or she dashed out in a crazy boat on the wide ocean to win with the dredgers the spoils of the oyster beds that lie on its bosom; the daintier fare was for the unhappy guest, and daily did she wander among the rocks, when the tides were retiring, for the shell-fish which they had flung among the fissures in their retreat, which she bore, exhausted with fatigue, to her home—and which her lovely child, now rising into womanhood, prepared for the luxurious meal; it was wonderful too, the settled prudence of the little maiden, who spoke nothing of the food which was borne from their frugal board; if she suspected the secret of her mother, she respected it too much to allow others to discover that she did so.

Many sad hours did Ruth pass in the robber's cave; and many times, by conversing with him upon the subject of her destiny, did she seek to alleviate the pangs its recollection gave her; but the result of such discussions were by no means favourable to her hopes; Rhys had acknowledged that his threat had originated in malice, and that he intended to alarm and subdue, but not to the extent that he had effected: "I knew well," said he, "that disgrace alone would operate upon you as I wished, for I foresaw you would glory in the thought of nobly sustained misfortune; I meant to degrade you with the lowest; I meant to attribute to you what I now painfully experience to be the vilest of the vices; I intended to tell you, you were destined to be a thief, but I could not utter the words I had arranged, and I was struck with horror at those I heard involuntarily proceeding from my lips; I would have recalled them but I could not; I would have said, 'Maiden, I did but jest,' but there was something that seemed to withhold my speech and press upon my soul, 'so as thou hast said shall this thing be'—yet take comfort, my own fortunes have ever deceived me, and doubtlessly ever will, for I feel as if I should one day return to this cave and make it my final home."

He spoke solemnly and wept—but the awful eye of his companion was unmoved as she looked on in wonder and contempt at his grief.

"Thou knowest not how to endure," said she to him, "and as soon as night shall again fall upon our mountains, I will lead thee forth on thy escape; the danger of pursuit is now past; at midnight be ready for thy journey, leave the cave, and ascend the rocks by the path I shewed thee, to the field in which its mouth is situated; wait me there a few moments, and I will bring thee a fleet horse, ready saddled for the journey, for which thy gold must pay, since I must declare to the owner that I have sold it at a distance, and for more than its rated value."

That midnight came, and Meredith waited with trembling anxiety for the haughty step of Ruth; at length he saw her, she had ascended the rock, and, standing on its verge, was looking around for her guest; as she was thus alone in the clear moonlight, standing between rock and sky, and scarcely seeming to touch the earth, her dark locks and loose garments scattered by the wind, she looked like some giant spirit of the older time, preparing to ascend into the mighty black cloud which singly hung from the empyreum, and upon which she already appeared to recline; Meredith beheld her and shuddered—but she approached and he recovered his recollection.

"You must be speedy in your movements," said she, "when you leave me; your horse waits on the other side of this field, and I would have you hasten lest his neighing should betray your purpose. But, before you depart, Rhys Meredith, there is an account to be settled between us: I have dared danger and privations for you; that the temptations of the poor may not assail me, give me my reward and go."

Rhys pressed his leather bag to his bosom, but answered nothing to the speech of Ruth: he seemed to be studying some evasion, for he looked upon the ground, and there was trouble in the working of his lip.

At length he said cautiously, "I have it not with me; I buried it, lest it should betray me, in a field some miles distant; thither will I go, dig it up, and send it to thee from B—, which is, as thou knowest, my first destination."

Ruth gave him one glance of her awful eye when he had spoken; she had detected his meanness, and smiled at his incapacity to deceive.

"What dost thou press to thy bosom so earnestly?" she demanded; "surely thou art not the wise man I deemed thee, thus to defraud *my* claim: thy friend alone thou mightest cheat, and safely; but I have been made wretched by thee, guilty by thee, and thy life is in my power; I could, as thou knowest; easily raise the village, and win half thy wealth by giving thee up to justice; but I prefer reward from thy wisdom and gratitude; give, therefore, and be gone."

But Rhys knew too well the value of the metal of sin to yield one half of it to Ruth; he tried many miserable shifts and lies, and at last, baffled by the calm penetration of his antagonist, boldly avowed his intention of keeping all the spoil he had won with so much hazard.

Ruth looked at him with scorn: "Keep thy gold," she said; "if it thus can harden hearts, I covet not its possession; but there is one thing thou must do, and that ere thou stir one foot. I have supported thee with hard earned industry, *that* I give thee; more proud, it should seem, in bestowing than I could be, from such as thee, in receiving: but the horse that is to bear thee hence tonight I borrowed for a distant journey; I must return with it, or with its value; open thy bag, pay me for that, and go."

But Rhys seemed afraid to open his bag in the presence of her he had wronged. Ruth understood his fears; but, scorning vindication of *her* principles, contented herself with entreating him to be honest.

"Be more just to thyself and me," she persisted: "the debt of gratitude I pardon thee; but, I beseech thee, leave me not to encounter the consequence of having stolen from my friend the animal which is his only means of subsistence: I pray thee, Rhys, not to condemn me to scorn."

It was to no avail that Ruth humbled herself to entreaties; Meredith answered not, and while she was yet speaking, cast side-long looks towards the gate where the horse was waiting for his service, and seemed meditating, whether he should not dart from Ruth, and escape her entreaties and demands by dint of speed. Her stern eye detected his purpose; and, indignant at his baseness, and ashamed of her own degradation, she sprung suddenly towards him, made a desperate clutch at the leather bag, and tore it from the grasp of the deceiver. Meredith made an attempt to recover it, and a fierce struggle ensued, which drove them both back towards the yawning mouth of the cave from which he had just ascended to the world. On its very verge, on its very extreme edge, the demon who had so long ruled his spirit now instigated him to mischief, and abandoned him to his natural brutality: he struck the unhappy Ruth a revengeful and tremendous blow. At that moment a horrible thought glanced like lightning through her soul; he was to her no longer what he had been; he was a robber, ruffian, liar; one whom to destroy was justice, and perhaps it was he—.

"Villain!" she cried, "thou—thou didst predict that I was

doomed to be a murderer! art thou—art thou destined to be the victim?" She flung him from her with terrific force, as he stood close to the abyss, and the next instant heard him dash against its sides, as he was whirled headlong into the darkness.

It was an awful feeling, the next that passed over the soul of Ruth Tudor, as she stood alone in the pale sorrowful-looking moonlight, endeavouring to remember what had chanced. She gazed on the purse, on the chasm, wiped the drops of agony from her heated brow, and then, with a sudden pang of recollection, rushed down to the cavern. The light was still burning, as Rhys had left it, and served to shew her the wretch extended helplessly beneath the chasm. Though his body was crushed, his bones splintered, and his blood was on the cavern's sides, he was yet living, and raised his head to look upon her, as she darkened the narrow entrance in her passage: he glared upon her with the visage of a demon, and spoke like a fiend in pain.

"Me hast thou murdered!" he said, "but I shall be avenged in all thy life to come. Deem not that thy doom is fulfilled, that the deed to which thou art fated is done: in my dying hour I know, I feel what is to come upon thee; thou art yet again to do a deed of blood!"

"Liar!" shrieked the infuriated victim. "Thou art yet doomed to be a murderer!"

"Liar!"

"Thou art—and of—thine only child!" She rushed to him, but he was dead.

Ruth Tudor stood for a moment by the corpse blind, stupefied, deaf, and dumb; in the next she laughed aloud, till the cavern rung with her ghastly mirth, and many voices mingled with and answered it; but the noises scared and displeased her, and in an instant she became stupidly grave; she threw back her dark locks with an air of offended dignity, and walked forth majestically from the cave. She took the horse by his rein, and led him back to his stable: with the same unvarying calmness she entered her cottage, and listened to the quiet breathings of her sleeping child; she longed to approach her nearer, but some new and horrid fear restrained her, and held back her anxious step: suddenly remembrance and reason returned, and she uttered a shriek so full of agony, so loud and shrill, that her daughter sprung from her bed, and threw herself into her arms.

It was in vain that the gentle Rachel supplicated her mother to find rest in sleep.

"Not here," she muttered, "it must not be here; the deep cave and the hard rock, these shall be my resting place; and the bedfellow, lo! now, he waits my coming."

Then she would cry aloud, clasp her Rachel to her beating heart, and as suddenly, in horror thrust her from it.

The next midnight beheld Ruth Tudor in the cave, seated upon a point of rock, at the head of the corpse, her chin resting upon her hands, gazing earnestly upon the distorted face. Decay had already begun its work; and Ruth sat there watching the progress of mortality, as if she intended that her stern eye should quicken and facilitate its operation. The next night also beheld her there, but the current of her thoughts had changed, and the dismal interval which had passed appeared to be forgotten.

She stood with her basket of food: "Wilt thou not eat?" she demanded; "arise, strengthen thee for thy journey; eat, eat, thou sleeper; wilt thou never awaken? Look, here is the meat thou lovest;" and as she raised his head, and put the food to his lips, the frail remnant of mortality shattered at her touch, and again she knew that he was dead.

It was evident to all that a shadow and a change was over the senses of Ruth; till this period she had been only wretched, but now madness was mingled with her grief. It was in no instance more apparent than in her conduct towards her beloved child: indulgent to all her wishes, ministering to all her wants with a liberal hand, till men wondered from whence she derived the means of indulgence, she yet seized every opportunity to send her from her presence. The gentle-hearted Rachel wept at her conduct, yet did not complain, for she believed it the effect of the disease, that had for so many years been preying upon her soul. Her nights were passed in roaming abroad, her days in the solitude of her hut; and even this became painful, when the step of her child broke upon it. At length she signified that a relative of her husband had died and left her wealth, and that it should enable her to dispose of herself as she had long wished; so leaving Rachel with her relatives in N—, she retired to a hut upon a lonely heath, where she was less wretched, because abandoned to her wretchedness.

In many of her ravings she had frequently spoken darkly of her crime, and her nightly visits to the cave; and more frequently still she addressed some unseen thing, which she asserted was forever at her side. But few heard these horrors, and those who did, called to mind the early prophecy, and deemed them the workings of insanity in a fierce and imaginative mind. So thought also the beloved Rachel, who hastened daily to embrace her mother, but not now alone as formerly; a youth of the village was her companion and protector, one who had offered her worth and love, and whose gentle offers were not rejected. Ruth, with a hurried gladness, gave her consent, and a blessing to her child; and it was remarked that she received her daughter more kindly, and detained her longer at the cottage, when Evan was by her side, than when she went to the gloomy heath alone. Rachel herself soon made this observation, and as she could depend upon the honesty and prudence of him she loved, she felt less fear at his being a frequent witness of her mother's terrific ravings. Thus all that human consolation was capable to afford was offered to the sufferer by her sympathizing children.

But the delirium of Ruth Tudor appeared to increase with every nightly visit to the cave of secret blood; some hideous shadow seemed to follow her steps in the darkness, and sit by her side in the light. Sometimes she held strange parley with this creation of her phrensy, and at others smiled upon it in scornful silence; now, her language was in the tones of entreaty, pity, and forgiveness; anon, it was the burst of execration, curses, and scorn. To the gentle listeners her words were blasphemy; and, shuddering at her boldness, they deemed, in the simple holiness of their own hearts, that the evil one was besetting her, and that religion alone could banish him. Possessed by this idea, Evan one day suddenly interrupted her tremendous denunciations upon her fate, and him who, she said, stood over her to fulfil it, with imploring her to open the book which he held in his hand, and seek consolation from its words and its promises. She listened, and grew calm in a moment; with an awful smile she bade him open, and read at the first place which should meet his eye: "from that, the word of truth, as thou sayest, I shall know my fate; what is there written I will believe." He opened the book, and read—

"*Whither shall I go from thy spirit, or whither shall I flee from thy presence? If I go up into heaven, thou art there; if I make my bed in hell, thou art there; If I take the wings of the morning, and dwell in the uttermost parts of the sea, even there shall thy hand lead me, and thy right hand shall hold me.*"

Ruth laid her hand upon the book: "it is enough; its words are truth; it hath said there is no hope, and I find comfort in my despair: I have already spoken thus in the secrecy of my heart, and I know that he will be obeyed; the unnamed sin must be—."

Evan knew not how to comfort, so he shut up his book and retired; and Rachel kissed the cheek of her mother, as she bade her a tender good night. Another month and she was to be the bride of Evan, and she passed over the heath with a light step, for the thought of her bridal seemed to give joy to her mother.

"We shall all be happy then," said the smiling girl, as the

youth of her heart parted from her hand for the night; "and heaven kindly grant that happiness may last."

The time appointed for the marriage of Rachel Tudor and Evan Edwards had long passed away, and winter had set in with unusual sternness even on that stormy coast; when, during a land tempest, on a dark November afternoon, a stranger to the country, journeying on foot, lost his way in endeavouring to find a short route to his destination, over stubble fields and meadow lands, by following the footmarks of those who had preceded him. The stranger was a young man, of a bright eye and a hardy look, and he went on buffeting the elements, and buffeted by them, without a thought of weariness, or a single expression of impatience. Night descended upon him as he walked, and the snowstorm came down with unusual violence, as if to try the temper of his mind, a mind cultivated and enlightened, though cased in a frame accustomed to hardships, and veiled by a plain, nay almost rustic exterior. The thunder roared loudly above him, and the wind blowing tremendously, raised the new-fallen snow from the earth, which, mingling with the showers as they fell, raised a clatter about his head which bewildered and blinded the traveller, who, finding himself near some leafless brambles and a few clustered bushes of the mountain broom, took shelter under them to recover his senses, and reconnoiter his position.

"Of all these ingredients for a storm," said he smilingly to himself, "the lightning is the most endurable after all; for if it does not kill, it may at least cure, by lighting the way out of a labyrinth, and by its bright flashes I hope to discover where I am."

In this hope he was not mistaken: the brilliant and beautiful gleam shewed him, when the snow shower had somewhat abated, every stunted bush and blade of grass for some miles, and something, about the distance of one, that looked like a white-washed cottage of some poor encloser of the miserable heath upon which he was now standing. Full of hope of a shelter from the storm, and, lit onwards by the magnificent torch of heaven, the stranger trod cheerily forwards, and in less than half an hour, making full allowance for his retrograding between the flashes, arrived at his beacon the white cottage, which, from the low wall of loose limestones by which it was surrounded, he judged to be, as he had already imagined, the humble residence of some poor tenant of the manor. He opened the little gate, and was proceeding to knock at the door, when his steps were arrested by a singular and unexpected sound; it was a choral burst of many voices, singing slowly and solemnly that magnificent dirge of the Church of England the 104th psalm. The stranger loved music, and the sombrous melody of that fine air had an instant effect upon his feelings; he lingered in solemn and silent admiration till the majestic strain had ceased; he then knocked gently at the door, which was instantly and courteously opened to his inquiry.

On entering, he found himself in a cottage of a more respectable interior than from its outward appearance he had been led to expect: but he had little leisure or inclination for the survey of its effects, for his senses and imagination were immediately and entirely occupied by the scene which presented itself on his entrance. In the centre of the room into which he had been so readily admitted, stood, on its trestles, an open coffin; lights were at its head and foot, and on each side sat many persons of both sexes, who appeared to be engaged in the customary ceremony of watching the corse previous to its interment in the morning. There were many who appeared to the stranger to be watchers, but there were but two who, in his eye, bore the appearance of mourners, and they had faces of grief which spoke too plainly of the anguish that was mingling within: one, at the foot of the coffin, was a pale youth just blooming into manhood, who covered his dewy eyes with trembling fingers that ill-concealed the tears which trickled down his wan cheeks beneath: the other—; but why should we again describe that still unbowed and lofty form? The awful marble brow upon which the stranger gazed, was that of Ruth Tudor.

There was much whispering and quiet talk among the people while refreshments were handed amongst them; and so little curiosity was excited by the appearance of the traveller, that he naturally concluded that it must be no common loss that could deaden a feeling usually so intense in the bosoms of Welsh peasants: he was even checked for an attempt to question; but one man—he who had given him admittance, and seemed to possess authority in the circle—told him he would answer his questions when the guests should depart, but till then he must keep silence. The traveller endeavoured to obey, and sat down in quiet contemplation of the figure who most interested his attention, and who sat at the coffin's head. Ruth Tudor spoke nothing, nor did she appear to heed aught of the business that was passing around her. Absorbed by reflection, her eyes were generally cast to the ground; but when they were raised, the traveller looked in vain for that expression of grief which had struck him so forcibly on his entrance; there was something wonderfully strange in the character of her perfect features: could he have found words for his thought, and might have been permitted the expression, he would have called it triumphant despair; so deeply agonized, so proudly stern; looked the mourner who sat by the dead.

The interest which the traveller took in the scene became more intense the longer he gazed upon its action; unable to resist the anxiety which had begun to prey upon his spirit, he arose and walked towards the coffin, with the purpose of contemplating its inhabitant: a sad explanation was given, by its appearance, of the grief and the anguish he had witnessed; a beautiful girl was reposing in the narrow house, with a face as calm and lovely as if she but slept a deep and refreshing sleep, and the morning sun would again smile upon her awakening:

salt, the emblem of the immortal soul, was placed upon her breast; and, in her pale and perishing fingers, a branch of living flowers were struggling for life in the grasp of death, and diffusing their sweet and gracious fragrance over the cold odor of mortality. These images, so opposite, yet so alike, affected the spirit of the gazer, and he almost wept as he continued looking upon them, till he was aroused from his trance by the strange conduct of Ruth Tudor, who had caught a glimpse of his face as he bent in sorrow over the coffin. She sprung up from her seat, and darting at him a terrible glance of recognition, pointed down to the corse, and then, with a hollow burst of frantic laughter, shouted—"Behold, thou liar!"

The startled stranger was relieved from the necessity of speaking by someone taking his arm and gently leading him to the farther end of the cottage: the eyes of Ruth followed him, and it was not till he had done violence to himself in turning from her to his conductor, that he could escape their singular fascination. When he did so, he beheld a venerable man, the pastor of a distant village, who had come that night to speak comfort to the mourners, and perform the last sad duty to the dead on the morrow.

"Be not alarmed at what you have witnessed, my young friend," said he; "these ravings are not uncommon: this unhappy woman, at an early period of her life, gave ear to the miserable superstitions of her country, and a wretched pretender to wisdom predicted that she should become a shedder of blood: madness has been the inevitable consequence in an ardent spirit, and in its ravings she dreams she has committed one sin, and is still tempted to add to it another."

"You may say what you please, parson," said the old man who had given admittance to the stranger, and who now, after dismissing all the guests save the youth, joined the talkers, and seated himself on the settle by their side; "you may say what you please about madness and superstition; but I know Ruth Tudor was a fated woman, and the deed that was to be I believe she has done: ay, ay, her madness is conscience; and if the deep sea and the jagged rocks could speak, they might tell us a tale of other things than that: but she is judged now; her only child is gone— her pretty Rachel. Poor Evan! he was her suitor: ah, he little thought two months ago, when he was preparing for a gay bridal, that her slight sickness would end thus: *he* does not deserve it; but for her—God forgive me if I do her wrong, but I think it is the hand of God, and it lies heavy, as it should."

And the grey-haired old man hobbled away, satisfied that in thus thinking he was shewing his zeal for virtue.

"Alas, that so white a head should acknowledge so hard a heart!" said the pastor; "Ruth is condemned, according to his system, for committing that which a mightier hand compelled her to do; how harsh and misjudging is age! But we must not speak so loud," continued he; "for see, the youth Evan is retiring for the night, and the miserable mother has thrown herself on the floor to sleep; the sole domestic is rocking on her stool, and therefore I will do the honours of this poor cottage to you. There is a chamber above this, containing the only bed in the hut; thither you may go and rest, for otherwise it will certainly be vacant tonight: I shall find a bed in the village; and Evan sleeps near you with some of the guests in the barn. But, before I go, if my question be not unwelcome and intrusive, tell me who you are, and whither you are bound."

"I was ever somewhat of a subscriber to the old man's creed of fatalism," said the stranger, smiling, "and I believe I am more confirmed in it by the singular events of this day. My father was a man of a certain rank in society, but of selfish and disorderly habits. A course of extravagance and idleness was succeeded by difficulties and distress. Harassed by creditors, he was pained by their demands, and his selfishness was unable to endure the sufferings of his wife and children. Instead of exertion, he had recourse to flight, and left us to face the difficulties from which he shrunk. He was absent for years, while his family toiled and struggled with success. Suddenly we heard that he was concealed in this part of the coast; the cause which made that concealment necessary I forbear to mention; but he as suddenly disappeared from the eyes of men, though we never could trace him beyond this part of the country. I have always believed that I should one day find my father, and have lately, though with difficulty, prevailed upon my mother to allow me to make my inquiries in this neighbourhood; but my search is at an end today—I believe that I have found my father. Roaming along the beach, I penetrated into several of those dark caverns of the rocks, which might well, by their rugged aspects, deter the idle and the timid from entering. Through the fissures of one I discovered, in the interior, a light. Surprised, I penetrated to its concealment, and discovered a man sleeping on the ground. I advanced to awake him, and found but a fleshless skeleton, cased in tattered and decaying garments. He had probably met his death by accident, for exactly over the corpse I observed, at a terrific distance, the daylight, as if streaming down from an aperture above. Thus the wretched man must have fallen, but how long since, or who had discovered his body, and left the light which I beheld, I knew not, though I cannot help cherishing a strong conviction that it was the body of Rhys Meredith that I saw."

"Who talks of Rhys Meredith," said a stern voice near the coffin, "and of the cave where the outcast rots?"

They turned quickly at the sound, and beheld Ruth Tudor standing up, as if she had been intently listening to the story.

"It was I who spoke, dame," said the stranger gently, "and my speech was of my father, of Rhys Meredith; I am Owen his son."

"Son! Owen Rhys!" said the bewildered Ruth, passing her hand over her forehead, as if to enable her to recover the combinations of these names; "and who art thou, that thus givest human ties to him who is no more of humanity? why speakest thou of living things as pertaining to the dead? Father! he is father to nought save sin, and murder is his only begotten!"

She advanced to the traveller as she spoke, and again caught a view of his face; again he saw the wild look of recognition, and an unearthly shriek followed the convulsive horror of her face.

"There! there!" she said, "I knew it must be thyself; once before tonight have I beheld thee, yet what can thy coming bode? Back with thee, ruffian! for is not thy dark work done?"

"Let us leave her," said the good pastor, "to the care of her attendant; do not continue to meet her gaze your presence may increase, but cannot allay her malady: go up to your bed and rest."

He retired as he spoke; and Owen, in compliance with his wish, ascended the ruinous stair which led to his chamber, after he had beheld Ruth Tudor quietly place herself in her seat at the open coffin's head. The room to which he mounted was not of the most cheering aspect, yet he felt that he had often slept soundly in a worse. It was a gloomy unfinished chamber, and the wind was whistling coldly and drearily through the uncovered rafters above his head. Like many of the cottages in that part of the country, it appeared to have grown old and ruinous before it had been finished; for the flooring was so crazy as scarcely to support the huge wooden bedstead, and in many instances the boards were entirely separated from each other, and in the centre, time, or the rot, had so completely devoured the larger half of one, that through the gaping aperture Owen had an entire command of the room and the party below, looking down immediately above the coffin. Ruth was in the same attitude as when he left her, and the servant girl was dozing by her side. Everything being perfectly tranquil, Owen threw himself upon his hard couch, and endeavoured to compose himself to rest for the night, but this had become a task, and one of no easy nature to surmount; his thoughts still wandered to the events of the day, and he felt there was some strange connection between the scene he had just witnessed, and the darker one of the secret caves. He was an imaginative man, and of a quick and feverish temperament, and he thought of Ruth Tudor's ravings, and the wretched skeleton of the rock, till he had worked out in his brain the chain of events that linked one consequence with the other: he grew restless and wretched, and amidst the tossings of impatient anxiety, fatigue overpowered him, and he sunk into a perturbed and heated sleep. His slumber was broken by dreams that might well be the shadows of his waking reveries.

He was alone (as in reality) upon his humble bed, when imagination brought to his ear the sound of many voices again singing the slow and monotonous psalm; it was interrupted by the outcries of some unseen things who attempted to enter his chamber, and, amid yells of fear and execrations of anger, bade him "Arise, and come forth, and aid." Then the coffined form which slept so quietly below, stood by his side, and in beseeching accents, bade him "Arise and save her."

In his sleep he attempted to spring up, but a horrid fear restrained him, a fear that he should be too late; then he crouched like a coward beneath his coverings, to hide from the reproaches of the spectre, while shouts of laughter and shrieks of agony were poured like a tempest around him: he sprung from his bed and awoke.

It was some moments ere he could recover recollection, or shake off the horror which had seized upon his soul. He listened, and with infinite satisfaction observed an unbroken silence throughout the house. He smiled at his own terrors, attributed them to the events of the day, or the presence of a corse, and determined not to look down into the lower room till he should be summoned thither in the morning. He walked to the casement, and looked abroad to the night; the clouds were many, black, and lowering, and the face of the sky looked angrily at the wind, and glared portentously upon the earth; the *sleet* was still falling; distant thunder announced the approach or departure of a storm, and Owen marked the clouds coming from afar towards him, laden with the rapid and destructive lightning: he shut the casement and returned towards his bed; but the light from below attracted his eye, and he could not pass the aperture without taking one glance at the party.

They were in the same attitude in which he had left them; the servant was sleeping, but Ruth was earnestly gazing on the lower end of the room upon something, without the sight of Owen; his attention was next fixed upon the corpse, and he thought he had never seen any living thing so lovely; and so calm was the aspect of her last repose, that Meredith thought it more resembled a temporary suspension of the faculties, than the eternal stupor of death: her features were pale, but not distorted, and there was none of the livid hue of death in her beautiful mouth and lips; but the flowers in her hand gave stronger demonstration of the presence of the power, before whose potency their little strength was fading; drooping with a mortal sickness, they bowed down their heads in submission, as one by one they dropped from her pale and perishing fingers.

Owen gazed, till he thought he saw the grasp of her hand relax, and a convulsive smile pass over her cold and rigid features; he looked again; the eye-lids shook and vibrated like the string of some fine-strung instrument; the hair rose, and the head cloth moved: he started up ashamed: "Does the madness of this woman affect all who would sleep beneath her roof?" said he; "what is this that disturbs me—or am I yet in a dream? Hark! what is that?"

It was the voice of Ruth; she had risen from her seat, and was standing near the coffin, apparently addressing someone who stood at the lower end of the room: "To what purpose is thy coming now?" said she, in a low and melancholy voice, "and at what dost thou laugh and gibe? lo! you; she is here, and the sin you know of, cannot be; how can I take the life which another hath already withdrawn? Go, go, hence to thy cave of night, for this is no place of safety for thee." Her thoughts now took another turn; she seemed to hide one from the pursuit of others; "Lie still! Lie still!" she whispered; "put out thy light! so, so, they pass by and mark thee not; thou art safe; good night, good night! Now will I home to sleep;" and she seated herself in her chair, as if composing her senses to rest.

Owen was again bewildered in the chaos of thought, but for this time he determined to subdue his imagination, and, throwing himself upon his bed, again gave himself up to sleep; but the images of his former dreams still haunted him, and their hideous phantasms were more powerfully renewed; again he heard the solemn psalm of death, but unsung by mortals—it was pealed through earth up to the high heaven, by myriads of the viewless and the mighty: again he heard the execrations of millions for some unremembered sin, and the wrath and the hatred of a world was rushing upon him: "Come forth! Come forth!" was the cry; and amid yells and howls they were darting upon him, when the pale form of the beautiful dead arose between them, and shielded him from their malice; but he heard her say aloud, "It is for this, that thou wilt not save me; arise, arise, and help!"

He sprung up as he was commanded; sleeping or waking he never knew; but he started from his bed to look down into the chamber, as he heard the voice of Ruth loud in terrific denunciation: he looked; she was standing, uttering yells of madness and rage, and close to her was a well-known form of appalling recollection—his father, as he had seen him last; he arose and darted to the door: "I am mad," said he; "I am surely mad, or this is still a continuation of my dream." He looked again; Ruth was still there, but alone.

But, though no visible form stood by the maniac, some fiend had entered her soul, and mastered her mighty spirit; she had armed herself with an axe, and shouting, "Liar, liar, hence!" was pursuing some imaginary foe to the darker side of the cottage: Owen strove hard to trace her motions, but as she had retreated under the space occupied by his bed, he could no longer see her, and his eyes involuntarily fastened themselves upon the coffin; there a new horror met them; the dead corpse had risen, and with wild and glaring eyes was watching the scene before her.

Owen distrusted his senses till he heard the terrific voice of Ruth, as she marked the miracle he had witnessed; "The fiend, the robber!" she yelled, "it is he who hath entered the pure body of my child. Back to thy cave of blood, thou lost one! back to thine own dark hell!"

Owen flew to the door; it was too late; he heard the shriek—the blow: he *fell* into the room, but only in time to hear the second blow, and see the cleft hand of the hapless Rachel fall back upon its bloody pillow; his terrible cries brought in the sleepers from the barn, headed by the wretched Evan, and, for a time, the thunders of heaven were drowned in the clamorous grief of man. No one dared to approach the miserable Ruth, who now, in utter frenzy, strode around the room, brandishing, with diabolical grandeur, the bloody axe, and singing a wild song of triumph and joy. All fell back as she approached, and shrunk from the infernal majesty of her terrific form; and the thunders of heaven rolling above their heads, and the flashings of the fires of eternity in their eyes, were less terrible than the savage glare and desperate wrath of the maniac:—suddenly, the house rocked to its foundation; its inmates were blinded for a moment, and sunk, felled by a stunning blow, to the earth;— slowly each man recovered and arose, wondering he was yet alive;—all were unhurt, save one. Ruth Tudor was on the earth, her blackened limbs prostrate beneath the coffin of her child, and her dead cheek resting on the rent and bloody axe;—it had been the destroyer of both.

THE LORD
OF THE MAELSTROM

THE RAVEN

> "—Hell is empty,
> And all the Devils are here."
> SHAKESPEARE

Somewhere about the year 112, in winter or summer—we are not exactly prepared to say which—died Olave the Second, one of the early kings of Denmark; he was a "fellow of no reckoning," for he took no account of anything that occurred during his reign, except the making of strong drink, and the number of butts in his cellar. His majesty, it must be avowed, was in the presumptuous habit of forestalling the joys of heaven (we mean Odin's), that is to say, he impiously got drunk every day of his life, before the regular allowance of fighting, the customary number of enemies' broken heads, and his own orderly death upon the field of battle, bore testimony that he was properly qualified for such supreme enjoyment. Olave in his life was a happy fellow; for, never having been sober during one hour of it, he had not the misfortune to hear all the ill-natured things that his courtiers and subjects said of his enormities, behind his back, or when he was asleep. It must, however, be acknowledged that, even among the unscrupulous Danes, who were not at that period remarkable for their practice of sobriety, Olave was a filthy fellow: to this hour he is held up as a monument of brutality and stupidity, and the memory of Jeroboam, the son of Nebat, who made Israel to sin, was not more devoted to execration among the Jews, than that of King Olave the Second among the Danes. On his death-bed, however, when he could no longer swallow his usual enlivening potations, blue devils beset his nights, and conscience twitted him with his ill-spent days. He had never broken a head in his life, except by proxy; and how could he make his appearance in Valhalla without a skull to drink out of?—to knock at the gates of Valasciolf without a goblet in his hand?—The thing was impossible; it was clear he would be kicked through Asgard, and sent to fret in Nifthiem, where the burning claws of Loki would set fire to the good liquor incorporated with his being, and reduce him to the condition of an eternal, thinking cinder!— Miserable anticipations! he tried to weep; but water, which he had hitherto scorned, now scorned him, and absolutely refused to come at his desire: he shed tears of mead, which he caught in his mouth as fast as they fell, partly from fear lest Odin should remark them, and partly because he could not endure to see good liquor wasted.

But all things have an end—in this world at least—and so it was with the life and repentance of King Olave the Second; he died without the drinking-cup he had regretted so deeply, and before he had time to frame a decent apology to Odin for venturing into Valhalla without one. There was a world of business now to be done at the palace of Sandaal: a dead king to be buried, and two living kings to be crowned; for such was the will of the lamented Olave, that both his sons should succeed him. They were princes of very different characters, yet their father, it should seem, loved them equally, as he divided his dominions very fairly between them, to the no small disgust of the elder prince, Frotho, who, like the imperial Octavius, some years before, could not bear a divided throne. This worthy in character resembled, in no slight degree, his excellent father, of dozy memory, for he loved to drink much and fight little—more especially as his younger brother Harold had a decided vocation for the latter employment, and none at all for the former: to him, therefore, he left the charge of the glory of the Danish crown, while he, for the present, contented himself with drinking to his successes. This good understanding, however, between the princes could not last forever. Frotho was, after all, only half a drunkard, and therefore extremely sulky in his cups —more especially when his Queen Helga seated herself at his elbow to twit his courage with the heroic deeds of his brother. Queen consorts should not meddle with politics, they never do anything but mischief—and so it proved in this instance; for Frotho grew absolutely delirious, kept himself entirely sober for three whole days, buckled on his wooden target, put himself at the head of his troops, and, swearing to be revenged upon his brother, marched on an expedition to Jutland. The expedition neither answered his intentions nor expectations; the men of Jutland were too many for King Frotho, for, headed by Feggo (the murderous uncle of the philosophic Hamlet, whose father was prince only of this part of Denmark), they drove Frotho "home without boots, and in foul weather too," as Glendwr did, long afterwards, King Harry Bolingbroke. Frotho could not stomach this affront—the beating was hard of digestion: his subjects made mouths at him too, and mimicked a race whenever he appeared in public. So he sent his brother, King Harold, who was a fighter to the backbone, to chastise the Jutlanders, which when he had done most effectually, Frotho grew more angry still; he detested his brother, dreaded his popularity, feared his wisdom, and quivered at his anger—so he began to consider seriously how he might cleverly and quietly put him out of the way.

King Frotho had two counsellors, neither of whom ever agreed with the other in the advice they gave his majesty: the reason was tolerably obvious, for the one was an honest man, the other a rogue, and, like the Topaz and Ebene of Voltaire, they bewildered the unhappy monarch with the diversity of their opinions and advice. On this occasion, however, King Frotho troubled only the rogue for his, which he was pretty certain beforehand would not differ very widely from his own. Eric Swen was an unprincipled ragamuffin who hated Harold, because he had discovered that Harold hated his vices; and, as that prince had two sons who were rising into manhood, he shuddered at the prospect of two or three strict warrior reigns, which would certainly bring virtue into fashion: the prince had refused him, too, the hand of his sister, which, to make the refusal more bitter, he had bestowed upon his rival in the council and camp, Frotho's general, Haquin. All these offences were carefully summoned up, to inflame his ire against Harold, by the devil, in the shape of Frotho, who promised him—Heaven knows what—both on earth and in Valhalla, if he would only push King Harold from his share of the stool, and leave both halves of it to Frotho.

Notwithstanding all the provocations on both sides, the confederates were two or three whole years before they could "screw their courage to the sticking place," that is, to the pitch necessary for the murder of King Harold. They had sent fifty inconsiderable nobles, whom they had found troublesome, to Asgard, without ceremony; but Harold was a king and a warrior, and required a good deal.

"If we could but pour poison into his ear," said Eric; "Or into his cup," replied Frotho; "Or stab him in his sleep," said Eric; "Or coax him out hunting with us," replied the brother, "and give it to him quietly in the forest."

But none of these safe plans would answer;—so Frotho, accompanied by his sole and trusty counsellor, rode off for the forest, to find the cave where, tradition said, had resided, from the days of the "Avatar" of Odin, his enemy Biorno, the descendant of Lok, grandnephew of Surter, and first cousin to the Wolf Fenris and Serpent Midgard. Frotho, however well-disposed to beg the aid and advice of the sorcerer, by no means felt quite at ease when he considered the family to which he belonged: the wolf and the eternal earth-circling snake were known to bear no very great partiality to the race of Odin—and Frotho, they knew, if they knew anything, was a true son of their enemy. Still the Danish monarch trotted on with his squire till they reached the centre of the forest.

"After all, Eric," said his majesty, as they trotted on cozily together; "after all"—but, as an historian, I must make one observation here: you are aware, dear reader, that the Scandinavians of the year 112, and sometime after, did not use the same simple, plain, common-place sort of style which they have adopted to express their meaning now-a-days. If we may believe their own writers, they were always in alt, gave their commands in a kind of heroic prose, and carried on dialogues in a sort of rambling blank verse. It must therefore be obvious to you, dear reader, that I spare you their language, and only give you their sentiments, which, to the best of my humble ability, I will translate for you into decent colloquial English, the better to carry your patience through the long-winded history which I am preparing as a trial for it. But to return to Frotho the Fifth of Denmark.

"After all, Eric," said he, "I have perhaps no great reason to fear these ugly immortals: as I am going to consult their kinsman, and am withal very well disposed to put an end to the race of Odin (that part of it at least most devoted to him), I think they may be civil to me. My own son Sevald is the only member of the family I wish to preserve, and I may soon mold him to my own opinions. If the sorcerer will only dispose of Harold for me, or tell me how I may safely dispose of him, I shall not haggle on the terms of assistance; I will do anything to serve him or his, which may not interfere with my own safety, or rob me of the diadem I am so anxious to wear alone."

Eric was about to reply to his magnanimous master, but paused, half afraid, as he discovered they were really in the sorcerer's neighbourhood, for the yawning mouth of the cave was actually staring them in the face. Frotho, as became him, now took the lead, and marched dauntlessly forward, though not without a glance backward now and then to see if Eric was close behind him, and as any sound struck upon his ear that bore any resemblance to a hiss or a howl. At length, after many turnings and windings, he found himself in a cavern of large dimensions, broadly lighted by a huge iron lamp, suspended from the upper part of it. He turned round to make some remark to his patient tail-piece, but was petrified to observe that he had fallen to the earth stiff and insensible to everything around him. The Danish monarch's cheeks waxed pale, and his knees began to smite each other; nevertheless he grasped the hilt of his falchion, as a slight noise on the opposite side withdrew his attention from the insensible Eric Swen; there stood an old man of reverend aspect, mildly but steadily gazing upon the king: "Art thou he whom I have been so long taught to expect?" said the sorcerer; "art thou the king of the race of Odin, alone chosen by his invincible foe to render a service to the son of Lok, and deserve the everlasting gratitude of his children? If indeed thou art the appointed, I bid thee highest welcome, for the task decreed to thee hath been denied to the immortals, above whom the grateful Loki will raise thee."

Frotho recovered his spirits at this address; half his business was already done, for his wishes were anticipated. He had been so little accustomed to receive compliments from his subjects, that his opinion of his own endowments had not been particularly high; but now he began to think he had mistaken himself, and was really a much greater man than he had suspected. He readily promised obedience to the sorcerer, upon certain terms, and assured him of his assistance when and wherever it might be demanded. The magician then proceeded to inform him that he was himself a descendant of Lok, and an ally of the spirits of fire, those daring beings who had for so many thousand years waged war with various success against Odin and his warriors, and which warfare would not cease till the end of the world; when, during a night which was to last a year, there would be a general battle, in which Earth, Niftheim, and Asgard, would go to wreck, and the conquering party be elevated to a newer and more beautiful heaven in Gimle—while Nastrande, a still gloomier hell, would be made out of the fragments of the old one, for the accommodation of the party conquered.

"Balder!" exclaimed Frotho, starting at this part of the story —for he never liked to hear anything of the old hell, which he thought quite bad enough without the spirits troubling themselves about the creation of another; "but I thought, sir sorcerer, that the wicked alone would be punished in Nastrande, after the long night and battle of the gods; I thought—"

"Exactly so, my son," interrupted the sorcerer; "the wicked certainly; for the conquered *will* be the wicked—that is beyond dispute; but *who* will conquer is not so certain; perhaps Lok, perhaps Odin—each, as far as I see, have an equal chance; take part then with us, and share our danger and glories in the next world, and our certain assistance in this." To this world, then (as King Frotho had at present more business in it), he limited his wishes, and gave Biorno his steady attention as he proceeded in his narrative. "Odin," the magician continued to observe, "though utterly unable to chain entirely the powers of Lok, had just now decidedly the advantage; for he had a few hundred years before seized upon his eldest son, the unwary Surter, whom he had caught out of his own territories, and wedged him, in the shape of a raven, into an iron cage, there to remain till one of his own race, a kingly son of his blood, should release him:"—a condition from Odin probably implying an eternal punishment—as that divinity, who does not appear to have been as omniscient as he ought, never imagined any member of his house would have been found silly enough to fulfil it.

"Now then," continued the magician, "I have consulted the eternal powers, and find that thou, Frotho of Denmark, art the king destined to this wondrous deed, and its following union with the immortals." Frotho gave his assent to all and anything proposed; and the sorcerer immediately began his operations; he raised his ebon wand above his head, with many magical flourishes—turned himself rapidly round—then more slowly, pausing at each of the cardinal points, and calling north, south, east, and west, upon the tremendous name of Lok. At that sound, so terrible even to the ears of spirits, the thunder began to rumble and the fires of Niftheim flash through the gloomy cavern; something like music was heard, and, though the concert was hardly better than those performed by King Frotho's own band during his drinking orgies, yet as the voices (and they were many) solely employed their powers in singing his praises, and the approaching deliverance of the god by his means, his majesty was pleased to think nothing in heaven could be half so fine. Presently the earth shook, and the sides of the cavern rocked; Biorno pointed to the bottom of the cave—and Frotho beheld it, after a few violent convulsions, suddenly open, and disclose to his view an enormous raven in a gigantic iron cage.

"Behold," said the magician to him, "the prison of the immortal prince of fire!—in that shape he must remain a hundred thousand years, unless a kingly hand of the line of Odin shall restore him (by breaking the bars of his iron cage) to power and to liberty. Monarch of Denmark! Go—and success attend thee."

Frotho obeyed immediately; he made a desperate attack upon the iron cage, but failed in his intention of rending away its bars; he made many earnest efforts, but all in vain—the bars remained unbroken. The Dane paused in vexation—he was frightened and mortified—and, by the howls and groans which resounded on all sides of the cavern, it was evident the anxious spirits of Niftheim sympathized in his distress: Biorno too, afflicted beyond measure at the ill success of the enterprise, threw himself upon the earth, tore off his magical cap, plucked up his hair by the roots, and howled as loudly as the noisiest of them. This dismal sight drove Frotho desperate; he collected all his energies for one mighty pull, rushed upon the cage, grappled with the bars, and, in an instant, threw them at the sorcerer's feet, who sprung up like an elk to receive them. Frotho stood majestically silent, while an uproar, such as no human ear has ever heard since, began its diversions in the cavern; a thick black mist quickly filled its whole space, so that Frotho could but indistinctly distinguish the figures who made up the ball; millions of shadows were flitting about, and millions of voices were laughing, singing, shouting, groaning, and cursing. Midgard raised his glittering snaky head above the darkness and the shadows, and greeted the monarch with a cordial and complimentary hiss; wolf Fenris tried hard for a good-natured howl; and the grim Hela, their sister, the Queen of Death, tortured her ghastly face into a smile, as she capered nimbly backwards and forwards in the festival, animated by the thought of the many meals Frotho would furnish for her famished maw. But, at length, the immortals grew weary of their own noises—the infernal jollification came to an end—the mist cleared off—the fires went out—the uproar died away—and Frotho's courage returned to its half-bewildered master, who took heart once again to look about him. He was alone (to his great joy) with Biorno, except that, in place of the raven and his cage, there sat, reposing upon a light cloud, his beautiful brow diademed with his native element, the triumphant prince of fire, in all the pride of beauty and victory.

"Frotho, son of Olave," said the sweet voice of the spirit; "bravest among the brave, and wisest of the sons of Odin—what is thy will with me? Tax my gratitude, preserver; ask, and obtain thy wishes."

Frotho waited for no further encouragement, but directly stated his wishes to reign alone in Denmark, and sweep off all the collaterals of his house, who were such bars to his glory.

"Thy brother's life I give thee," said the spirit; "destroy him when thou wilt, but be cautious to keep it secret: his elder son shall in vain endeavour to oppose thee—I will baffle his claim, and proclaim thee sole monarch in Denmark; but touch not the life of Haldane; he has offended Lok, and the god demands the victim, whom he will receive from no mortal hand: for Harold the younger, do with him as thou wilt, but, if thou spare his life, he shall have no power to harm thee; go—reign—prosper—nothing shall do thee wrong till thyself shall fulfil a decree which is gone forth respecting thee; thou shall prosper till thy hand shall unite thy own blood to that of thy deadliest foe: beware of this, and triumph."

"Prince of the powers of Niftheim," said Frotho, "surely Harold, my brother, is my deadliest foe, and he has no daughter to whom I can give my son; but I will be mindful of thy words, and remember thy warning."

The spirit then desired him, should any event disturb his tranquility, to come to the cavern and strike thrice upon the side where stood the iron cage: "Biorno shall meet thee," continued he, "and yield thee, in my name, such help as thou mayest require;" then, slowly and silently encircling himself in the clouds which surrounded him, he gradually disappeared from the sight of Frotho, leaving the cavern illuminated only by the light of the iron lamp which hung from its centre.

Biorno, too, had vanished, leaving him alone with Eric Swen, who, now easily awakened from his trance, prepared to follow his master home, who simply informed his confidant that he had consulted the magician, who had advised the murder of Harold, and promised him success in its performance. This was readily undertaken by the profligate Eric, who, watching, with a lynx-like assiduity, his opportunity, plunged his sword in the heart of the unhappy Harold with such right good will and judgment, that the prince died before he knew he was wounded: nor was Frotho behind his confederate in the good management of a difficult affair, and skill in getting out of a dilemma; and this was especially proved, when the body of Eric Swen, transfixed by a well-aimed javelin, was found stark and stiff by the side of King Harold, and Frotho ordered everybody to believe that these enemies had fallen in single combat with each other.

There was one Dane in the court of King Frotho who took the liberty of believing contrarily to the royal orders; this was the brave Haquin, the brother-in-law of the two kings, and their favourite general and minister: he knew Frotho, and he suspected foul play. He secured the persons of his murdered master's two sons, and, giving out that Haldane should challenge his father's crown against Frotho, in an assembly of the states, retired from the court to his own towers, till the nobles should be pleased to appoint a day for hearing the claim of his ward. In the meantime, Haldane himself had not been idle; he employed a good number of his vacant hours in making tender love to his beautiful cousin, the young Ildegarda, and laying at her feet the crown which he *was* to have, and which Ildegarda accepted, as a thing of course; for she already considered herself the Queen of Denmark. Haldane was tenderly beloved, and they each looked forward to the day on which he was to claim his father's crown from the ambitious Frotho, as that which was to seal their love and their happiness.

That day at length arrived; the states, the nobles, the warriors, and a great part of the troops, were assembled in an open plain, where Frotho, on his throne, awaited the arrival of his kinsman. His majesty had arrayed himself with peculiar splendour for this solemn occasion; his long hair, now slightly tinged with grey, floated down his back, while all his face was clean shaven, except his upper lip, which exhibited a most magnanimous mustache; his breast, arms, and legs were painted in the brightest blue, and the most fashionable pattern in Denmark; a short petticoat of lynx skin, fastened round his waist by the paws of the animal, descended to his knees; and from his shoulders to his heels, secured round his neck by claws of gold, fell the robe of royal magnificence, the mantle made of the skins of many ermines; his feet were defended by shoes of the sable of the black fox; his neck was ornamented by a chain of gold, and the regal circle of the same precious metal shone through his locks around his temples; on his left arm was a target of leather, studded with brass nails of unusual brightness and immense value; in his right hand he held the sceptre; he sat upon a throne covered with the hides of wolves, and over his head floated, in proud sublimity, the standard of Denmark, the raven.

People may talk as long as they please about innate dignity and the majesty of mind, but the majesty of fine clothes has a much greater influence upon popular opinion—else wherefore that elderly proverb which sayeth that "fine feathers make fine birds?" Everybody knows that King Herod's silver petticoat made the stupid mob of Judea mistake him for a god; and on this day, so important to Haldane, Frotho's amazing magnificence made *his* people mistake him for a hero. So strong ran the tide of popular opinion, that when Haldane, simply habited, mounted on his snow-white steed, and only attended by Haquin and a few of his father's friends, rode up the area, they scarcely deigned (though he was rich in all the pride of youth and graceful beauty) to consider him worth looking at: all eyes were turned to Frotho's painted waistcoat and superb ermine cloak; and Haldane also beheld, with extreme disgust, that all his own friends, and the warriors favorable to his claims, who had fought by his side under his father's banner, had been carefully excluded from the council, which he beheld supplied by the creatures of his uncle; he saw that his cause was lost before he could say a word: he was not daunted nevertheless; he demanded his right from Frotho, who, refusing to admit his claim, was challenged by the youth to decide the quarrel on the spot.

"The states and the troops are present," said the prince; "let them be witnesses of this combat, which thy ungenerous ambition must render mortal: if thou desirest a double crown, shew that thou knowest how to defend it; descend from thy throne, meet me fairly, and let Denmark be the reward of the conqueror."

Slowly, very slowly, King Frotho rose from his throne, for he saw that something was expected of him: although not precisely a coward, he had no mind to encounter his nephew, whose feats of arms he well knew; and earnestly and anxiously he put up a prayer to Surter to remember his promise, and baffle his kinsman in this trying emergency. Surter was not deaf; for scarcely had the monarch put forth one leg for the purpose of descending from his throne, ere a wonder attracted the attention of the whole assembly; the sound of rushing wings was heard from a distance, and slowly, sailing steadily through the clear air towards his point, appeared a gigantic raven: black as the shining locks of Odin was the magnificent and stately bird, who, tranquilly passing over the multitude, suspended himself in air over the head of Frotho, and, hovering steadily above him, clapped his enormous pinions in triumph. Haldane suspected a trick—Haquin was startled—but the multitude beheld a miracle, and the will of Odin clearly expressed by his own particular messenger: the bird hovered in the air a few moments, to witness the general acknowledgment of Frotho, then, amidst the deafening shouts of the people, ascended slowly upwards, cleaved through the clouds, and vanished.

Haldane stood apart, during the scene, in proud contempt of the ingratitude of his people; and the multitude were making too terrific an uproar to allow his few friends one word in his favour. Frotho, pleased by the timely aid of Surter, was grateful for the first time in his life; and, remembering the commands of the spirit, abstained from taking what he yet scarcely knew how to spare, the hated life of Haldane. Assuming an air of paternal interest and kindness, he bade the young prince retire from his presence and kingdom, without fear of molestation.

"Son of my brother," said he, "seek another kingdom for thy rule, this the gods have given to Frotho; retire peaceably, and take with thee what part of my treasure thou wilt."

"The crown, then," boldly replied the prince; "for what is there, traitor! in thy power to bestow, that is not already mine by right? No! mean-souled coward! I scorn thy courtesy, and I defy thy anger."

But this gallant resistance availed nothing in a lost cause; his own party counselled him, for the present, to get out of the reach of Frotho's javelin; and, too wise to disdain advice alike given by friends and enemies, he obeyed their wishes, and, after taking a tender leave of his betrothed Ildegarda, and promising to claim her as a king, withdrew to Sweden to solicit aid from its warlike monarch in defence of his title—aid which he did not receive; for King Frotho soon after received notice that he had been murdered on that inhospitable coast soon after his landing, and, as it could never be ascertained by whom, Frotho silently congratulated himself upon the sure and ready vengeance of his ally and divinity, Surter. Haquin, alarmed by this circumstance, and more than ever suspecting the honesty of King Frotho, withdrew from court with the young Harold, now the sole surviving son of his murdered master, and, proclaiming him lawful king of Denmark, set up his standard in the heart of the country. Many powerful nobles, disgusted by the cruel brutality of his uncle, immediately joined him; and Frotho, frightened by danger into valour, and relying upon the promises of Surter, put himself at the head of his troops, and prepared for a civil war.

Many skirmishes took place between the hostile powers, though nothing very decisive occurred; but the troops of Frotho had generally the advantage, and always when the king commanded in person. Joy of this discovery nearly upset his majesty; he began to think himself a great general as well as a gallant warrior: he got exceedingly drunk with some of his old cronies who had made the discovery, and, during the deep sleep which followed this little extravagance, Haquin attacked his camp, beat his generals, carried off his son Sevald a prisoner, and nearly seized upon his sacred majesty himself, who knew nothing at all of the matter. Poor Sevald was marched off for the camp of the enemy, in a transport of sorrow and despair.

"Be not offended, prince," said the good Haquin to him when he was brought before him in his tent—"be not offended that the chance of war has placed thy person in my custody for a season; it is no dishonour to be the prisoner of Haquin. Our war is with thy father, not with thee; and should Harold succeed, even to the slaying of his uncle, he will never wrong thee, but yield thee thy just right, a second throne in Denmark: be not disturbed therefore at the slight accident of this war."

This was kindly meant, but it entirely failed in its purpose, and Sevald would have still continued to grieve if he had not discovered that fair princesses are better comforters than old soldiers. He learned that his lovely cousin Ildegarda was in the camp of her father, and he concluded that things were not quite so bad as they might have been. Sevald admired his fair kinswoman extremely, and, as Haldane's death had set her free, he worked out the prettiest little romantic scheme possible for putting an end to the horrors of civil war and restoring peace to

Denmark: he determined to entreat his father to give him Ildegarda for his bride, to adopt Harold as his partner, and thus to
reconcile all parties to his ascendancy; but, unhappily for poor
Sevald's delightful scheme, all the persons concerned in it were,
though for different reasons, materially against it. Ildegarda,
true to the memory of Haldane, would listen to no second love
—Haquin, faithful to the cause he had adopted, would rather
have consigned his daughter to the grave than to the arms of a
son of Frotho—and the Danish monarch would entirely have
lost the little wit he possessed, at the bare possibility of such a
destructive union as that of his own blood with that of his deadliest foe, for such now had the father of Ildegarda become to
him. When he did hear it, he grew absolutely wild with terror
and rage; he imprecated the most deadly curses upon his son,
should he venture to espouse his cousin; and flew off like a
madman to the cave of Biorno in the forest, to consult him in
this most desperate emergency. He found the sorcerer at home,
and willing to assist him, which he civilly did by the best advice
in his power; he desired him to return to his camp and attack
the troops of Haquin, promising to commit that leader, his
daughter, and Prince Sevald, safely into his custody; at the same
time hinting that, as Surter had done as much for his friend as
could decently be expected, he need not call upon him for
further assistance, which, unless from his own imprudence, he
would not need, and Loki had prohibited them from supplying.
Frotho thanked him for past favors and present services, and,
promising to demand nothing more for the future, they parted
good friends, though not to meet again in this world at least,
whatever might happen in the other. Frotho had no sooner
reached his camp, than he hastened to profit by his friend's
advice, and instantly experienced its salutary effects; he
defeated his antagonists in a pitched battle, recovered his son
Sevald, and, to his infinite joy, possessed himself of the persons
of Haquin and his daughter, though Harold escaped in the

battle, and hid himself securely from the pursuit of his enemy. Had Frotho followed the suggestions of his own cruel heart, he would have decided Haquin's destiny at once by taking off his head; but, fearful of his nobles, who held the chief in high esteem, and having likewise no hope of discovering Harold, except through his friend, he resolved to spare his existence, but to keep him in close imprisonment with his daughter, whose influence over Sevald he still dreaded, and whom, as the daughter of his sister, he dared not injure farther. The poor prince wept bitterly over his ruined hopes, and Frotho rejoiced at the delightful consummation of his: he enjoyed himself in his own way, killing and drinking by turns—till, in a fit of madness and extravagance, he impiously declared that he had a Valhalla of his own, which he would not change for Odin's, upon any terms that divinity could offer. Everything was happiness in the palace, and Frotho was the most mischievous and merry of kings.

THE ISLE OF THE MAELSTROM

"What have we here?
a Man or a Fish?
—Legged like a Man,
and his fins like arms."

SHAKESPEARE

*E*very sweet hath its sour," saith a very respectable old ballad—and truly there is wisdom in the saying. King Frotho's sanctity, as a crowned prince of the holy race of Odin, became at this period, for the first time, somewhat of an inconvenience to him. In the midst of his festivities, howls and cries penetrated to his palace, and reached his ears, though surrounded by buzzing flatterers, and rendered dizzy by strong potations. His people of Norway were unhappy, and they called upon their common father to relieve their misery. A pest had arisen among them which no one could conquer, for no one knew how to attack: the frightful whirlpool of the Maelstrom had a guest, and the desolate island of Moskoe an inhabitant; it was neither man, beast, bird, nor fish, that had taken up his residence in this part of his Danish majesty's dominions, but a most extraordinary compound monster, possessing all the faculties of each of these several creations. As he had his little island entirely to himself, the want of society suggested to him an expedient by way of amusement, and also of remedying this evil —he employed his leisure in making descents upon the Norwegian coast, and carrying off the grown inhabitants, four or five at a time, and the little children by dozens, whom he devoured with as little remorse as he would young rabbits or dried herrings. The people were terrified, and the nobles began to bestir themselves; they sent out armed men in well-built boats, headed by an able leader, and desired them to bring in the monster prisoner; but the lord of the Maelstrom, so far from being brought to consent to this arrangement, exactly reversed the orders of the Norwegian ministry, for he sunk all their boats, and carried their crews' prisoners to his island. Frotho heard this pitiful tale with much indifference, till they besought him to go in person against their enemy, well knowing that no magic or infernal power could succeed against the race of Odin —then he sprung up in alarm, and declining, in his own person, all pretensions to superior sanctity, sent one of his best generals with a band of his own chosen troops, in two gallant vessels, to seize or destroy the monster. All Norway assembled on the coast to witness their success; they saw the ships sail gallantly on, and, on the opposite coast, the giant monster rush into the waves to meet them. With a strength against which they could not contend, he seized the luckless vessels, drew them coolly and steadily on to the frightful gulf of the Maelstrom, and then, swimming back to his island, left the noble ships to be sucked into the frightful bosom of the gulf. The waves swept over them, and the tale of their deeds was told.

Frotho was frightened into sobriety when this news reached him; Denmark became as clamorous as Norway in the matter, and he was compelled to promise that he would exert his sanctity, and go in person to the attack of the monster: but he delayed as long as he possibly could, and, under pretense of making preparations, gave the fiend of the Maelstrom time to eat half the children in Norway. At length "delays became dangerous" even to Frotho himself; he was obliged to depart, and, well armed, well-guarded, and well attended by a resolute band of the bravest of his nobles and chiefs, set sail, on a fine sunny day, for the desolate isle of the Maelstrom. His magnanimous majesty could not, however, help shivering at the first glance of the island; but he took courage, on remarking that the beast did not come out to meet him, nor advance to the attack as in the former instance; so he landed in good spirits on the island, promising himself immortal glory in his conquest. A sufficient band was left in charge of the vessels, and Frotho, with his chiefs, went boldly forward into the island.

In the first few miles there was nothing to astonish them; rugged rocks, a roaring sea, and desolate naked heaths, were all that greeted the travellers: they had expected nothing else, for the Moskoe was well known to most of the party, and had never been suspected of sheltering a paradise in its bosom. Such, however, to their boundless astonishment, the heroes now found to be the case. A beautiful country arose amidst the desolate isle; and, after the first five miles, hills, dales, fertile valleys, richly wooded groves, and sparkling rivers, said a thousand smiling good-morrows to the travellers. The scene was too charming to terrify, else the total absence of anything like human inhabitants might have been sufficient to startle King Frotho, and make him doubt whether all was as it should be in this particular part of his dominion. There was a total silence around them, unbroken, save by the sweet warblings of birds, or now and then the light foot of the flying deer, as, scared by the clatter of their arms, they fled from them into the forests. Thus they proceeded till they arrived before the gates of a majestic palace of black marble, whose open portals courteously invited them to enter. Frotho paused—so did his nobles; it was finer than anything in Denmark; infinitely larger, grander, bolder, blacker, than the palace of Sandaal, the royal residence of King Frotho himself—so that it was clear no human hands had reared it: but whose hands had?—a puzzling question, which King Frotho would not take upon himself to answer.

But the portals stood invitingly wide open, and King Frotho was waxing weary; so, without any further debate or permission demanded, they marched into a stately hall, where invisible cooks had made successful preparation for a magnificent supper; Frotho looked and longed. There was venison, noble venison of the flesh of the elk, roasted wild boar, and a cistern of excellent fish delicately stewed in whale fat; there was a bowl of hydromel, in which King Frotho might have been drowned, and another of milk, that might have served him for a bath—in short, the temptation was too great for the tempted; and though King Frotho well knew the danger incurred, even by a son of Odin, in tasting enchanted food, yet he could not resist the whale fat and the hydromel.

"The monster certainly expected me," said he to his attendants.

"He is willing to make his peace with you," said they to the king.

"It would be uncivil not to taste his good cheer," said the master.

"Let us shew that we accept his submission," replied the servants. So they all sat down with one accord to the feast, and ate, and drank, and were merry.

The bowl of hydromel was empty—Frotho was looking into it disconsolately with one eye (for the other was asleep), and growing angry with his nobles, who had assisted him too heartily, and been over-zealous in obeying his commands to pledge him to the health of their entertainer. After grumbling and growling for some time over the huge and now dismal-looking bowl, his majesty took it into his head to be displeased with the inattention of his host, who had failed to remark and replenish, as he ought to have done, the empty bowl of departed hydromel.

"Lord beast of the island," said his majesty, at length, having thought till his thirst grew intolerable; "lord beast of the island, I will permit thee to be viceroy in Moskoe, but thou must not spare thy hydromel when thy master deigns to visit thee. For thy good cheer, I thank thee; thy meat is of the best, and abundant, but, by the burning wheel on Balder's breast, thy drink was scanty; and I command thee hither to supply me with more."

A rumbling of thunder and a long terrific howl was the answer to the speech of the monarch. Frotho shivered with affright, for he thought he recognized, amid the uproar, the voices of his old acquaintances the illustrious snake and wolf, cousins of his sorcerer friend Biorno; and, as he was a little diffident of their conduct, notwithstanding his services to Surter, he did not altogether relish the meeting, under present circumstances; so, ensconcing himself in the centre of his gallant little band of valiant warriors, he patiently awaited what was to be the second part of his entertainment. This was settled in an instant; neither Fenris nor Midgard broke upon the supper party of the monarch, but a being more horrible than either, and infinitely more hideous than his or any imagination had already conceived of the monster of the Maelstrom gulf. A stern gigantic shape entered the hall, and stood steadily face to face with King Frotho and his nobles: his features were frightfully flat, and two sunken fiery eyes shot terrific glances from a visage almost entirely covered with dark and grisly hair; long black elf locks hung down upon his shoulders, huge teeth grinned through his grisly beard, and his fingers and feet were furnished with claws which were worthy of Nebuchadnezzar himself; his enormous body was covered with black bear-skins, so disposed as to serve him for a whole suit; and his huge hand grasped a monstrous club, which seemed very desirous of a nearer acquaintance with his majesty of Denmark's brains. The monster contemplated the group for a moment in silence; he suffered them even to draw their swords and advance exactly one step towards him, when he suddenly lifted his terrible club, and, without striking a single blow, laid them all prostrate at his feet. He then approached King Frotho; the son of Olave shrunk from the uplifted club, and bellowed out, in terror and haste, that he was the King of Denmark. "And thy errand?" said the monster. King Frotho was silent. "I know it," observed the spectre; "and for its presumption, but for one thing which I expect of thee, would bind thy trembling feet for ever to the spot where thou standest staring at me. Hark thee! thou fool of Surter's making! who hopest to overcome the invincible by human arms—hear, and obey what I shall command thee. I do not hate thee, and would not harm thee, for thou art the friend of Lok; but my wrath against the kingdoms must be appeased, and my divinity acknowledged. I demand thy daughter. A spotless virgin of royal blood must come voluntarily hither to be sacrificed on this island, and thou must conduct her: do this, and henceforth I too am thy friend; neglect it, and my thunders shall shake thy palace of Sandaal, and this club dash out thy brains and scatter them over thy sovereign throne."

King Frotho looked aghast—not at the condition of his safety, but his utter inability to fulfil it—there was no cheating such an enemy as this—so he told him the plain truth, that he had no daughter, and humbly apologized for the want of one. The monster yelled at him, and again lifted up his club. Frotho,

in agony, besought him to have pity, and then suddenly recollected that he had a niece who was his prisoner, and whom he
very readily offered to his disposal. The monster hesitated—at
length, in reply to Frotho's earnest entreaties, he consented to
spare his life, upon condition that, in the space of twenty days,
he should land the princess on the island, and deliver her safely
into his hands, to be sacrificed by his own high priest in his
palace; and promising, should Frotho fail in his engagement, on
the very next day, to shake Sandaal about his ears, and dish up
his carcass as a meal for Midgard. Frotho sealed his promise
with a solemn oath, and the monster dismissed him with a kick
on the throne-honouring part of his person, which sent him not
only through the palace gates, but one mile forward in his
journey to the coast, which long before he had gained, his
panting train overtook him, being driven out by the lord beast,
to wait upon and console their disgraced and afflicted master.

King Frotho had no intention, rogue as he was, to cozen the
Moskoe monster; on the contrary, he was desirous to obtain his
friendship and forbearance towards his subjects and the little
Norwegian children for whom he had evinced such cannibal
prepossessions. He was not sorry, either, so effectually to
dispose of Ildegarda, whose union with his son he had such
good reason to fear. The difficulty would be to persuade the
princess to go voluntarily to be eaten. He was ingenious
however—naturally fertile in expedients—and he soon hit upon
a method of persuasion which he deemed infallible: he told the
poor princess that the monster demanded her or her father as
prisoners; that he allowed her to choose, and if she thought
proper to decline, he should ship off old Haquin immediately, to
be stewed in whale fat, and served up for supper with milk
sauce, according to the pleasure of the monster, in the marble
palace of Moskoe: for his own part, in relation to herself, he
pretended he did not clearly understand to what the lord of the
island had destined her, but he hoped nothing so terrible as a

roast or a hash. Ildegarda wept, but came into the scheme quicker than Frotho had anticipated. Haldane was dead, and her father's life in danger; by the sacrifice of her own, which was now really become indifferent to her, she could at least preserve the last of these beloved beings, and therefore she did not hesitate. Making Frotho swear a tremendous oath (which she knew no Dane dared break), to release her father on his return from Moskoe, she prepared to accompany the king, and, in less than twenty days, Frotho and his beautiful victim landed on the island, and prepared to march to the black palace alone.

They had not proceeded far on their journey, when their progress was arrested by the appearance of a singular cavalcade coming to meet them; this consisted of a magnificently painted chariot, drawn by four snow-white reindeer, each of whom, to the astonishment of Ildegarda, had feet of pure gold: behind it came the monster-man himself, mounted upon a coal-black steed of extraordinary size and beauty, who pawed the earth impatiently, and, snorting and foaming as he reared, threw his magnificent mane from side to side, as if weary of the slight restraint which his rider appeared to impose upon him—the latter had now a bear-skin cap upon his head, on the top of which sat a monstrous raven, decorating it by way of crest; and another on his wrist, with infinite grace and gravity, seemed ready to serve him in quality of falcon extraordinary.

The cavalcade paused on remarking the strangers; and the grim monster, advancing to Frotho, sternly demanded, "Comes the maid willingly?"

"She does," replied Frotho; "and"—But the monster no longer gave him any attention: he did not even look at Ildegarda, but, bending his head down towards his horse's ears, gravely and mildly asked, "Steed of heaven, art thou weary?"

"No," replied the horse, "but I have today been so long upon the earth, that its gross air is beginning to affect me—the sod is heavy to my feet, and somewhat checks my swiftness: let me relieve my legs, I pray thee." The strange monster nodded his grisly head in reply, and Frotho beheld the courser slowly and deliberately drew up his four black legs, and let down three white ones in their places.

The king began now to guess his company; "It is the wondrous steed of Odin," said he in a whisper to Ildegarda; "the immortal eight-legged Sleipner: but what is he who rides him?"

The princess had no time to answer this question, even had she been able, for the monster seemed determined to have all the conversation to himself.

He spoke to the raven on his head: "Hugin," said he, "take the reins, guide my reindeer smoothly, and conduct the lady to the palace: and you, Munin," added he to the bird on his wrist, "hasten homewards, and see that all be prepared for the victim."

At these terrible words, the tears of Ildegarda began to flow, and Frotho prepared himself to make a speech. The monster heeded neither the one nor the other, but nodded to Ildegarda to ascend the chariot, which when she had done, he turned round to Frotho, lifted up his terrible club, and exclaimed, in a voice of thunder, "Go!" It was but one word, but the tone and the action weighed more than five hundred with Frotho, who, fearing to hear it repeated, darted from the party, and set sail for Denmark without once looking behind him.

In the meantime, Ildegarda was conducted by her ill-looking escort to the marble palace, and left by him in the same hall in which Frotho had rested on his first arrival: here, too, she found a supper prepared for her, though in a somewhat different taste from the former; but the princess had no inclination to eat—indeed she felt determined not to be fattened before killing, and threw herself upon the earth in a paroxysm of grief and despair. Suddenly, soft and sweet music broke upon her ear, and the beautiful voice of some holy unseen thing thus sung soothingly to her sorrow:—

When the thunder-bolt cleaveth
The trembling sky—
When the mad ocean heaveth
His wild waves on high—
When the coiling snake waketh
From the heaving earth curled,
And upreareth and shaketh
An agonized world—
When his coil thrice he foldeth
Around the night-born,
Till the gazer beholdeth
Red blood fill her horn—
When Valkyries scatter
The clouds which they tear,
And their steed hoof's loud clatter
Is heard in the air—
When on oak tops the tramping
Of their hoofs echo loud,
While their snorting and champing
Is lost in the cloud—
When wizards are breaking
The sleep of the dead,
And the shadows are waking
From each gory bed—
When the dog of hell howleth,
As the sheeted dead glide
Where the Queen of Death scowleth,
Grim Fenris beside—
When Surter assembleth
The lost round his throne—
Then the murderer trembleth,
And the murderer alone.
But then, guiltless beauty,
What hast thou to fear?

All owe thee their duty,
All homage thee here;
The life thou hast given
The immortals will claim;
And Rinda in heaven
Stamps thy star-written name.

The princess listened in breathless astonishment, and, when the sweet sounds died away, spoke in cheerful tones to the friendly singer.

"Thanks, gentle magician," said she aloud; "I submit to the pleasure of Odin, and will not be ungrateful for thy anxiety; see, I will partake of thy hospitality, and then retire to rest confident in thy gracious protection."

Ildegarda then ate something of the repast, and the moment she had concluded, the dishes and bowls retired of themselves from the table, without any assistance, through the doors and windows of the palace. While she was lost in astonishment at this singular attendance, the doors on the opposite side of the hall opened of themselves, and she, supposing it a summons for her attention, immediately passed through them, and heard them close behind her. She traversed several stately rooms, till at length she stood in one more magnificent than the rest, and which, from the circumstance of the doors closing when she entered it, she concluded was designed by her host for her chamber. Grateful for his indulgence, she determined to accept his courtesy, and threw herself down upon her couch to sleep: satisfied, she reviewed the events of the day, and found she had little reason to complain.

"I could even be happy," said Ildegarda, "if I were assured of the safety of my father."

The wish was instantly gratified; a large curtain on the opposite side was suddenly withdrawn, and, represented on a magic mirror, the princess beheld her father in his own palace, conversing earnestly with his attendants. The vision lasted but a few moments—the curtain fell again before the mirror, and Ildegarda, in a transport of gratitude, thanked aloud the courteous monster, who thus sought, as he had promised, to offer her the homage most pleasing to her feelings.

Ildegarda now tried to compose her spirits to sleep—the pale moon had risen over the island, and was pouring a flood of calm cold light into each apartment of the palace—suddenly, her beams were eclipsed by a light so glorious that the senses of the princess ached as she contemplated the wonder; she looked up to discover the cause, but mortality drooped under its excess of glory, and she bent downwards towards the earth; a soft voice called upon her name, but the princess could not reply; then the beautiful being, who was resting upon the light, beheld the embarrassment of her beloved, and, dismissing part of the effulgence by which she was surrounded, stood visible to the mortal sight, and Ildegarda beheld her beloved goddess, the guardian of her youth, the divine object of her innocent worship, the radiant Rinda, the daughter of the sun, the beloved of Odin and Freya.

Ildegarda bent her brow still lower to the earth, and kissed the fringe of the mantle of her goddess; then the most lovely of those lovely beings, who float on their ether thrones round the domes of Valasciolf, spoke tenderly to the fairest of her worshippers.

"Thou hast done well and wisely," said the daughter of heaven to the child of earth, "in thus offering thy life for thy father and thy country, and thou hast not disappointed my hope; I carried up the perfume of the holy deed to the foot of the throne of Odin; pleased, he took it from my hand, clothed it in light, and placing it on a branch of Hydrasil, the tree of heaven, bade it blow and expand into an immortal flower, to commemorate thy virtue, and remind him of thy deserving.

Child of my love—hope all—fear nothing—endure with patience—and thy reward shall be most glorious."

The goddess then recalled around her the extended beams of light, and, concentrating their brightness round her person, again became insupportably effulgent to human vision; in the next instant she was gone, and the glory she had left died away when unfed by her presence.

How sweet was the sleep of Ildegarda that night, and how blessed was her awakening on the morrow! Morning, the gay bride of Balder, beheld her descend joyfully to the hall, after adorning her lovely person with an elegant dress, selected from many, which the unseen hands of her watchful attendants had placed in her apartment for that purpose. Arrived in the hall, she expressed a wish to breakfast; and instantly the courteous dishes glided in from doors and windows to the table, attended by a grave-looking bowl of milk, which steadily sailed on till it placed itself in the centre, where it remained till the princess, by rising from table, dismissed its services for the present. She then roamed through the vast gardens of this beautiful place, and talked to the birds and the deer, fondly hoping and expecting that they were enchanted princes and princesses, and, like the black horse whom she beheld on her arrival, endowed with the faculty of speech; but, after much conversation on her own part, she was compelled to resign this pleasing illusion, and believe that they were merely real birds and real deer, who could only sing and leap. She then returned to the palace, wandered over its spacious apartments, and amused herself by counting the passages and doors. Still the day went off heavily, even with the aid of these time-killing pastimes; and when the hour of supper arrived, the princess welcomed it as sincerely as if hunger had been the instigator of the pleasure her countenance expressed; she seated herself at the table, and was earnestly and anxiously employed in coaxing the birds to partake of it—when a loud clap of thunder shook the palace to its foundation, and terrified all appetite from the poor princess. She had hardly time to think of its cause, ere it became apparent, for the monster-man himself entered the hall, and, clad in his customary dress, stood still in the middle of the apartment. Although his appearance was as usual, yet his manner was entirely different, for his step was slow and irresolute, and his voice mild and timid; he scarcely ventured to look up as he asked, in a humble and supplicating manner, if the princess would permit him to pay his duty while she supped. Ildegarda, somewhat re-assured by his gentleness, requested him to use his pleasure in a place where unquestionably all things were at his disposal.

"Not so, gracious lady," replied the courteous monster; "I will not stay in your presence, but with your express permission: my power I cede to your beauty and virtue, and am content myself to be the first subject of so lovely a sovereign."

This gallant speech was made with so much humility and respect that Ildegarda was not alarmed by its tenderness; and the monster, to shew (after she had granted permission) how highly he valued this trifling favor, and how little he was disposed to encroachment, declined the seat which, after a struggle, she offered him, and seated himself upon the ground, at a considerable distance from her. Touched by this humble homage and generous delicacy of a being so powerful, and at whose mercy she so entirely was, the princess so far conquered her abhorrence, as to present him with food and drink; the former he declined, but he took the again-summoned bowl of milk from her snowy hand, and, with a gesture of respectful gratitude, tasted the balmy liquor, as if to indulge her wish. At length, after a long silence, he asked her if she could be happy on the island?

"I hope so," replied the princess; "but will you tell me, sir sorcerer, what has thus singularly changed my destiny? I came hither to die—yet I live—and anxiety is even manifested by my enemy for my happiness. How am I to understand these contra-dictions?"

"Call me not your enemy, beautiful Ildegarda," replied the monster, "for that I have not been; destiny had decreed you to be a victim, though not of death; I am but its instrument to work out its intentions; the sacrifice of your liberty only was demanded, and your generous resignation of life itself has impelled me to love your worth, and lighten, as far as my power will, the burthen of your sorrows. I cannot release you from this rock, but I can surround you with pleasures, and render your bondage supportable."

Ildegarda was pleased with this explanation, and, after thanking her host for his generous intentions, withdrew to her chamber, though not till she had accorded to Brandomann (for that he had told her was his name) permission to attend her on the next evening to supper: this was an honour she would gladly have declined—but she felt it would be ungracious, and that he had some right to calculate upon her complaisance. The next night came, and Brandomann was punctual—conducting himself in the same timid manner—though, observing the dislike of Ildegarda towards him, he put an end to the interview earlier than usual, and quitted her presence in sorrow. The princess was sad that she had inflicted pain, yet she could not but hope that the hideous being would not again seek her soci-ety. In this she was disappointed—he came at night, as before, and seated himself silent and sorrowfully at her feet; he spoke not, and scarcely ventured to look at her, till she, affected by his griefs offered him the bowl and bade him drink; he took it with a smile—the poor monster intended it so, but the frightful grin which distorted his features was so odious, that Ildegarda sick-ened with affright, and heartily repented her condescension. Brandomann understood her disgust.

"Ildegarda," he said, mournfully, "I too well know how justly I must be an object of abhorrence to the eye of beauty; I will not give you pain therefore—though it will destroy the only happiness I have ever enjoyed, I will intrude no more into your presence—I will not destroy the little felicity which fate has left you."

He arose to retire; but the generosity of the princess overcame her reluctance—she was not proof against this noble self-denial—and, rising hastily from her seat, she requested, entreated—nay, commanded him to continue his visits. Brandomann was but too happy to obey; and he retired comforted from her presence. The next night Brandomann was not so silent—he exerted himself to amuse and interest his lovely prisoner; and he succeeded admirably when he spoke of the present state of Denmark—the disorders of the king—the disappearance of both the princes, sons of Harold—and the courage and integrity of her noble father; upon this theme he discoursed till tears of pleasure filled the eyes of the princess, whom he repeatedly assured of Haquin's safety.

"Should you wish a confirmation of the intelligence which I give you," continued Brandomann, "on the first day of every month examine the magic mirror in your chamber; it will satisfy your curiosity, by representing your father and his employments; but only at that time must you consult it."

Still Brandomann continued to talk, and Ildegarda to listen, till she forgot to wish for the hour of separation, and even suffered the monster to retire first; the next day she grew weary ere evening, and waited with something like impatience for the supper hour: it came at last, and Brandomann with it, who perceived, by the reception she gave him, that he was no longer so unwelcome a guest as formerly. Animated by this belief, he again exerted all his powers to interest the princess; he related to her the early history of her country, and the exploits of the greatest heroes, her ancestors of the race of Odin; he then went on to discourse of the Scaldres, their singular union, their mystic occupations, and their magnificent poems; he himself, he remarked to her, was of this privileged order, and, without wearying her attention, recited some of his own compositions and those of his noble brethren. Ildegarda was charmed by his discourses. Balder had touched his lips with eloquence, and Brage had rendered his voice melodious, and many words flowed over his lips, sweet, yet powerful, as a torrent of silvery waters. The princess was pleased while she only listened—when she looked, the spell was broken.

THE GUESTS

"Misery acquaints a man with strange Bedfellows."

SHAKSPEARE

*D*ay after day thus glided on without much variation, though not so heavily as formerly.

One evening Brandomann said to her, "Your mornings must still be wearisome to you; perhaps it might give you pleasure to travel around this little island; when such shall be your wish, summon aloud your carriage, with the snow-white deer (that which brought you hither), and it will instantly attend your command."

The princess was impatient, till the next morning gave her an opportunity of indulging this new pleasure—for when our pleasures are few, every little variation is hailed as a new one— she sprung lightly from her couch, and, with beaming eyes and a throbbing heart, ascended her chariot, which, at her wish, waited at the gates of the marble palace. For some hours she was delighted to be borne swiftly by the coursers of light through flowery vales and blooming gardens; but at length grew weary of the silence and monotony which everywhere

surrounded her, and the inability to utter or reply to an observation. The deer looked at her with their intelligent eyes, and
seemed to understand her feelings.

"Yes, turn then, my lovely deer," she replied in answer to
their silent interrogatory; "bear me again to my home."

She entered the marble hall. It was many days since she no
longer startled at the clap of thunder which announced the
approach of Brandomann, and now she heard it with pleasure.

"You have been amused today," said he to her as he entered.
"Not much," she replied; "although I blush to say so; I would be
happy if I could, yet I cannot help feeling that solitude is
melancholy."

"Alas! yes," replied the lord of the Maelstrom; "but there are
companions to whom it is preferable. If I did not fear offending
by my presumption—"

He was eagerly interrupted by Ildegarda, who accepted the
embryo offer with delight; and her manner had such an effect
upon the monster, that again the princess repented her condescension. He made ample amends for his hideous joy, however,
on the following day, when attending Ildegarda on her journey,
by his timid and gentle modesty. Mounted on his coal-black
steed, he respectfully followed her brilliant chariot, and never,
except in answer to her summons, ventured to approach her
side. The princess was naturally generous, and this conduct
secured her confidence. She now encouraged him to converse,
called him frequently to her side, and took pleasure in calling
forth and listening to his observations.

On their return to the palace, a huge raven flew down from a
tree upon the shoulder of Brandomann, and whispered something in his ear; the latter immediately turned to Ildegarda:
"Princess," he said, "the only friends who ever enliven this solitude by visiting me, are now on the island; will you permit them
to attend you at supper?"

Ildegarda consented joyfully: the thought of once more

seeing human beings filled her spirit with rapture; and, hastening to her apartment, she spent the intervening time in dressing her lovely person to the utmost advantage, not only for her own sake, but also to do honour to the taste and generosity of Brandomann, who had been most lavish in his preparations for her toilet. At length she descended, and, with a palpitating heart, entered the hall. At the door she was met by Brandomann himself, who courteously led her forward to present her to his guests—they rose to receive her—but imagine the astonishment of Ildegarda!—No words can do justice to her surprise, as she surveyed the assembled party: neither knight nor lady, spirit nor fiend, greeted her entrance—but on one side stood an enormous wild boar—on the other a beautiful white she-goat—in front stood the eight-legged steed of Odin—and the two ravens, whom she had seen on her landing on the island, had perched themselves with infinite gravity upon Brandomann's club. The princess turned to her friend, and was about to demand an explanation, when she was prevented by the beautiful goat, who, with an air at once kind and dignified, welcomed her to the island, which she said was happy under the government of the good Brandomann, the favourite of Odin, and whom all good spirits loved: the boar made her his best bow—Sleipner assured her of his devotion—the ravens were happy in the honour of her acquaintance—and Ildegarda, after replying to each of these extraordinary visitors, recovered something of her composure, and smilingly sat down to supper with her company. She was about to apologise for the want of proper fare, when she beheld them supplied with their own particular dishes by the same unseen attendants who so assiduously waited upon her. Oats and hay, in a silver manger, were placed before Sleipner—a huge tray of nuts and acorns sallied in, and stood stationary at the tusks of the boar—a salad was the supper of the white goat—and a raw rump steak was provided for the accommodation of the ravens. The princess began to be amused with her situation and company, and listen to their conversation with considerable interest: Munin and Hugin, the raven messengers of Odin, were talking over some of the divinities of Asgard; and Sleipner mentioned a journey which Thor the Thunderer intended shortly to take upon his back, to correct the impious inhabitants of Jutland, who, since the ascension of the murderer Feggo to his brother's throne, had totally neglected his worship.

"Is the murdered prince in Asgard?" demanded Brandomann.

"He has a magnificent palace in Valasciolf," replied the huge boar, "where he resides among the other heroes and the divine family and ministers of Odin, and with them usually spends his nights at the banquet in Valhalla; but he is not a favourite warrior there: if he was no more amiable on earth than he is in heaven, I am not surprised at his wife's wishing to get rid of him. Hamlet is also there, and almost as unpopular as his father. Can you imagine it possible, he spends all his time with Forsete at Glitner, and has grown so wise and disputatious, that he is continually instructing Odin himself; nay, the other morning, just before the sounding for the combat, he spoke so learnedly to that blind Horror, whom we dare not name out of heaven, and who is already sufficiently inclined to mischief, that Thor, provoked, lifted up his mallet to knock out the shadow of his brains—but Balder interfered, and his eloquence and Lofna's smile restored peace to heaven."

"And how go on the happy Scaldres?" demanded Brandomann; "what is become of the unlucky Hiarn, whose skill in singing gained him a crown?"

"He is singer-in-chief in Valhalla," replied Sleipner; "and indeed his strains well deserve this distinction. But see," he continued; "the princess looks to you for an explanation: take your harp, Brandomann, and let it tell the story of Hiarn."

"I obey you," replied the lord of the Maelstrom; and he caught up his harp and sung—

THE LEGEND OF HIARN

The heart of the monarch was savage and wild,
And his red hand with lifeblood was gory;
He spared not the matron, he spared not the child,
Proud youth, nor the head that was hoary.
Then Hiarn arose—and his melody's voice,
As over the wild harp it swept,
Brought relief to the land, bade its nobles rejoice,
For the dark monarch listened—and wept!
And his sorrow was holy, for into his heart
Those tones tender pity had flung—
And Fate whisper'd, "Thy soul shall with music
*   depart"—*
So he died, while the sweet harper sung.
Then Hiarn was king—for the fierce nobles came
Subdued by his powers alone,
They crowned his bright brow, proclaimed his great
*   name,*
And lowlily knelt at his throne.
Then Hiarn was king, and—

"Alackaday!" said the boar, who did not appear to have any very great taste for music, and who was beginning besides to be weary of Brandomann's dismal ditty; "alas! for the poor harper; it is a pity, after such a glorious opening, the close of his history should have been so dismal."

"What was it?" demanded Ildegarda; "tell me, I pray you, what was the fate of Hiarn?"

"A prince of the blood," replied the courteous boar, "the

warrior Fridleff, who did not understand music, challenged the crown from Hiarn: he was too good a musician to make anything but a contemptible soldier, so, as might have been expected, he sunk under the first blow of Fridleff. But, grieve not for him, charming princess, he is well rewarded for his short period of suffering; a throne in Asgard—a palace dome in Valasciolf—are surely higher blessings than even reigning in Denmark—"

"Serimnor!" said the white goat, interrupting the conversation, and pointing with her horns to the stars, which were now rapidly gemming the heavens; "see, the lights in the palaces of Asgard are lit—the deities and heroes are on their way to Valhalla—let us not keep them waiting, but hasten to supper, lest we should offend the Highest by our presumption."

Thus saying, she departed, after a friendly good night to the princess, and a promise to spend many evenings with her in the island. Serimnor, deeply engaged at that moment in a dispute with Brandomann about the politics of Jutland, did not remark her departure, but was reminded of it, to the no small astonishment of Ildegarda, in a very extraordinary manner; a gigantic pair of hands, the right brandishing an enormous carving knife, coolly entered the folding doors, and, seizing the throat of the luckless Serimnor, without any sort of notice or preparation, cut it from one side to the other, just as he was pronouncing the names of Harwendil and Feggo, which, from the suddenness of this maneuver, burst through the gaping orifice in his throat, instead of by the usual channel of communication—the mouth. The terror of Ildegarda, who had begun to esteem the polite and obliging Serimnor, was greatly increased by the extraordinary coolness of Brandomann, who stood looking on as if nothing particular had happened, and only discontinued his speech when the body of the poor boar was dragged from the apartment by the murderous pair of hands. It seemed as if the whole party had been in a conspiracy to frighten the timid Ildegarda; for, on the disappearance of the boar, Sleipner started up, and, snorting till fire darted from his nostrils and eyes, sprung up into the air, and pawing, and dashing, and foaming, ascended up to the clouds through the roof of the palace, which parted to give him passage—while the two ravens flew screaming out of the window. Brandomann had disappeared in the bustle, and, as he did not attend her on the following morning, she waited with much uneasy impatience for an explanation in the evening: this was given by the good-natured boar himself, who had marked her anxiety, and hurried first to the palace in order to relieve it.

He thanked her for the interest she took in what appeared to be his suffering; "But grieve not, loveliest of maidens," said the gallant beast, "at an event which is to me but the consummation of my glory: every night thus I die without pain, and my flesh is served up to the banquet of the gods—while my spirit enjoys a blissful sleep, from which it awakes in the morning to animate the same form in which it was clothed the day before. The beautiful goat whom you saw is the immortal Heidruna, whose milk is the hydromel served up to the table of Odin. She alone, last night, was punctual to her engagement, while the rest of the party, enchanted by your beauty, forgot the hour, and had some difficulty to reach Valhalla in time to avoid the reproach of Odin."

Scarcely was this explanation given, ere Heidruna herself entered, attended by the ravens and Sleipner, who apologised for their hasty departure the evening before; and a moment after, the clap of thunder announced the approach of Brandomann. The whole party now sat contentedly down to supper, infinitely pleased with themselves and each other; and perhaps it would have been difficult to find one more happy, or its members bearing more sincere goodwill towards each other. The next day was the first of the month, and the princess hastened to avail herself of the magic gift of Brandomann. With intense anxiety she raised the curtain, and her heart throbbed with delight to behold her father in health and spirits, well-armed, and travelling, attended by a band of gallant warriors, who appeared to be anxious for his safety. Ildegarda looked at him with rapture, and new feelings of gratitude to Brandomann gave the evening which followed this happy morning, fresh charms in her eyes, and made her confinement in the desolate island, with none but the ugliest of orangutangs for a constant companion, no longer either gloomy or dreadful.

One morning, while surveying together the beauties of the island in a sentimental walk, Brandomann asked the princess if she had now entirely resigned herself to the lot of total seclusion in the island of the Maelstrom.

"I may, and do sometimes regret the halls of my fathers," replied the tender Ildegarda. "But when I reflect from what miseries my devotion has preserved my beloved country, and still more beloved father, I feel that I ought not to complain. Neither am I insensible of what I owe to you; and I acknowledge that, without any other motive, your generous protection of me and care of my happiness deserves the sacrifice even of these regrets: I am willing to make it, and should even rejoice in an opportunity that would allow me to convince you of my sincerity."

"You have, then (and permit me to say I hope it), banished from your heart the remembrance of Haldane?" said the monster.

"Alas! no," replied Ildegarda, bursting into tears of tenderness at his recollection; "that can I never do; and it is the certainty of his loss that enables me so well to support this destiny: but do not let this disturb you—the recollection of Haldane will never interrupt my gratitude to you."

"And you could resolve upon fresh sacrifices if they were demanded of you?" inquired Brandomann.

"I could," replied the princess.

Brandomann paused—he looked sadly and earnestly at Ildegarda, and then, as with a violent effort, flung himself at her feet, and tremblingly demanded, "Princess, will you become my wife?"

A shriek of horror, and a look of unmeasured abhorrence, was the only reply of the hapless Ildegarda; and too plainly these tokens spoke to the unfortunate Brandomann. He calmed his agitation—arose from her feet, and spoke kindly and steadily to tranquillize hers.

"Do not hate me, beautiful sovereign of my destiny," said he, "that thus I am compelled to add to your inquietudes. Yet be not alarmed needlessly; I adore you, but no force shall be put upon your inclinations: forgive me, if, impelled by a power I dare not disobey, I am sometimes obliged to give you pain by this question. But fear not—my wishes shall be sacrificed to yours—I would not receive that hand, dear as it would be, unless voluntarily presented by yourself."

The princess took courage at this declaration of her hideous lover. She knew he was a monster of his word; and she thought if he would not receive her hand till she presented it, she should be safe from the infliction of such a husband. Assuring him, therefore, that she was far from hating him, and expressing with warmth the sentiments she really felt for her grim admirer, the poor monster was somewhat comforted, which Ildegarda was not sorry to remark; for if Brandomann was ugly when he was gay, he was ten thousand times more so when in sorrow. They returned to the palace in tolerable spirits, and in the evening Ildegarda took an opportunity of depositing her perplexities in the bosom of the respectable white goat, for whom she began to experience something of filial affection. Heidruna consoled the princess by her unqualified praises of the honour and sincerity of Brandomann, and her firm conviction that Ildegarda would never be molested by his fondness; although Heidruna thought, and could not help telling her young friend, that in the world she might have matched herself with many a greater beast than Brandomann: but, as this was entirely a matter of opinion, she rather soothed the princess than contradicted her. The good Serimnor interrupted the *tête-à-tête*, and fully seconded the opinion of Heidruna, both as to the honour and goodness of the lord monster of Moskoe.

"You observe," said he to Ildegarda, "that he has been admitted among the Scaldres, an order which generally requires perfection from its aspirants; and great must his virtues be, when the unbounded ugliness of his person could not outweigh them, nor conceal the richness and beauty of his mind. He is also, as we are, the descendant of Odin, and peculiarly favored by the mightiest of the gods, and his son Thor, the thunderbolt: he enjoys extensive power, and many prerogatives not granted to the more beautiful children of nature, to compensate for the imprisonment of such a spirit in so hideous and detestable a frame. Were it possible to overcome your natural repugnance, you would have no reason to regret the change; but should your aversion be invincible, you will have nothing to fear, since he will continue to you the tenderest and humblest of lovers, and we shall always remain your friends."

The princess thanked the friendly boar for his kind assurance, and they separated for the night in increased good will towards each other. In a few days after this conversation, Brandomann sought the princess in her chamber.

"A storm is gathering above the whirlpool," said he; "its effects will be terrific—our friends are collected to watch its progress—shall we follow them to the coast? If it will interest you, I will raise my magic tent upon the top of the highest rock, and, sheltered even from the slightest drops of rain, you shall see the storm in its terrors, and the fiend's unseen of mortal eyes, who increase its horrors and sport in its bosom."

Ildegarda accepted the invitation, and the reindeer swiftly bore their light and lovely burthen to the rocks, accompanied by Brandomann, whose eight-legged steed would far have outstripped the nimble coursers of the princess, but for the frequent checks of his rider. Arrived at the point of rock, they beheld the waters raging around them (for the island was seated in the midst of the gulf), but with less violence than Ildegarda had expected: she remarked this to her attendant.

"The waters are now at their height," replied Brandomann; "and for one quarter of an hour it will be tolerably calm, but the power of the storm will be tremendous when that short interval shall be past: many, deceived by the calm, venture out while it lasts, and encounter certain destruction at its close."

Ildegarda continued watching for the termination of the delusive calm, when her meditations were interrupted by the arrival of Heidruna, Serimnor, and the ravens: they arranged themselves round the chariot of the princess, and, protected from the storm by the magic tent of Brandomann, stood watching its progress in silent anxiety. The deceitful calm, as the lord of the island had predicted, was of no long duration. In a few minutes the brightness of Balder was entirely obscured; the wind chorus began, and swept low and sullenly over the waters, which now rose upwards, gently murmuring, as if they were the echoes of the distant song.

"Listen, Ildegarda," said Brandomann; "to you it is given to hear the secrets and wonders of the earth, in recompense for being thus shut out from its more social intercourse: listen, and you will hear the unknown song of the winds: hark! how it rises from an immeasurable distance, and yet you can distinguish their voices, and the words they utter. Now they come nearer —hush!"

THE SONG OF THE WINDS

From the couch of the billows,
The hollow bed
Where ocean pillows
His giant head—

From secret caves,
Where ancient Night
Sleeps secure
From staring light—
From the breast
Of the trembling earth,
Scorning rest,
We have our birth.
Up, up, upward, murmuring,
Up, up, upward, still go we.
From wild Hecla's burning cells,
Where the giant mother dwells,
Who to Lok, in days of yore,
Sin and death and horror bore—
From the geyser's boiling springs,
We soar, upborne on rushing wings,
Singing louder as we go,
Blow, ye wild winds, louder blow!
Up from the Dolstein still rise we,
Where about us rolled the sea,
And beneath, forever whirled,
The master spirit of the world—
From the raging Dofrefeld,
Where green Niord's feast is held—
From the land of eternal snow,
Blow, ye wild winds, louder blow!
We come, we come! The forests wave,
As above their tops we rave.
Blow winds, blow! the crashing tree
Of our might shall the witness be;
The staggering ship, and the broken mast,
Heaving, rended, sinking last;
And the crash of falling towers,
Speak our presence, and our powers.

Blow winds, blow! to heaven ascending,
Clashing, crashing, crushing, rending,
Wrath on earth and ocean pouring,
O'er the scared world, raging, roaring.

"The storm is indeed terrific now," said Ildegarda; "I can almost see it in the air, as it scatters the clouds before it: look how the waters rise to meet it, roaring with the fury and force of a cataract!"

Amid the uproar, she thought she distinguished other noises than those of the tempest—a sound like the howls and shrieks of pain: she noticed the circumstance to Brandomann.

"You are right," he replied; "look yonder, where a desperate battle is waging, in despite of this scene of tempest. A bear has swum from his mountain territory of Hilseggen to prey upon the flocks of Suarven, one of the few islands in this gulf which is inhabited; a single gallant shepherd has attacked him, but I fear the bear has the mastery: see! the shepherd has lost his staff, and the monster grapples with him closely—he hugs him fiercely!— Is there no way by which I can save him? What, ho! shepherd!— what, ho!—loosen yourself from the grasp of your enemy and fly—stand on the very edge of the rock, and let him spring against you!—So, so—the fellow fears me no less than the bear, yet he obeys—he is crouching—his enemy runs—plunges—ah! ah!—he has lost his balance and dashes headlong into the stream —well, run, shepherd!—He stays not to sing the death-song for his foe.—Good night, friend bear, you will sup with the fish of the Maelstrom tonight!"

While they looked on, they beheld the savage animal strug- gling for his life against the dreadful current, but in vain; borne onward, despite of his roaring, he was soon over the terrible pool, and then whirled rapidly round, till he was sucked down into the bosom of the dismal gulf, which, sages have written, penetrates the globe. Ildegarda pitied the poor bear, whose love of mutton had occasioned him so miserable a fate; but a new wonder now claimed her attention and diverted her thoughts from his sorrows: this was another island, slowly arising from the bottom of the lake, and covered with sea-weeds, becoming stationary at no great distance from Moskoe. Before Ildegarda could point it out to her companions, Serimnor advanced hastily towards Brandomann.

"There is mischief abroad, dear brother," said he; "this storm is not of Niord's raising. Some friend beloved of Odin, and abhorred of Lok, is certainly in danger; for look who are sporting in the tempest."

He pointed to the bosom of the gulf and to the rocky shore of Otterholm. In the centre of the one, Ildegarda beheld the head of a monstrous serpent reared above the waves, and surveying with fiery eyes the distant sea; and on the other a hideous wolf, with his attention fixed in the same direction, and howling in concert with the storm. The princess shuddered, and, for the first time in her life, drew nearer to Brandomann for protection.

"You have nothing to fear, dearest," said he, "from these monsters whom you behold; they are indeed your foes and mine, for they are the children of Lok, and the enemies of Odin; but they have no power over you, and mine, by the gift of their conqueror, is greater than their own. He whom you see in the waters is the giant snake, whose folds of sin encircle the guilty earth, and who now, from its centre, is bidding defiance to some noble foe of his evil father. Fenris the wolf-dog, guard of hell, appears only when mischief is in the air, to increase, by his cries and the horror of his form, the fears and the danger of his victim. I deem some hapless vessel has approached too near this coast during the calm, and now the storm will drag it to destruction. But let us watch—Hugin and Munin, stretch out your pinions—fly over the waters, and tell me what you descry."

The messengers of Odin obeyed—they flew over the bosom

of the lake—then out towards the boundless and ungirt ocean: suddenly they returned.

"A sail! a sail!" said Hugin.

"A gallant ship!" cried Munin; "the whirl has surely caught her, she comes on so rapidly."

Soon, very soon, she neared, and drove onwards, visible to all. Brandomann grasped his club: "Some bold adventurers," said he, "doubtless, who seek to land upon this island in defiance of the will of Odin; if so, they are lost indeed, for the King of Valhalla has resigned them to the power of the infernals."

It was frightful to mark the force with which the ship drove on.

"They make for the island which has just risen from the lake," said the princess.

"Death will too surely greet them there," replied Brandomann; "for that is no land, but the snare of fiends to beguile; it is the dreadful Kraken, that monster of the deep, who, when the vessel touches him, will sink, and draw it with him—"

And the vessel was near the monster, when a piercing shriek from Ildegarda arrested the thoughts of Brandomann.

"It is my father!" she cried—"it is my father!—I know his banner—he seeks me on this island—have mercy, Odin!—Oh, Brandomann, if thou lovest me"—"If I love thee!—lo! now I disobey the will of Odin for thee!—judge, then, how dear thou art!"

He started from her side, sprung upon Sleipner, darted from the rock, and the next instant Ildegarda beheld his giant form stemming the torrent with a power equal to its own. The wolf beheld him and ran howling away, while a single blow from his mighty club drove the grim serpent beneath the waves, to howl his disappointment in Niftheim.

Ildegarda heard none of the consoling speeches addressed to her by her friends; her ear—her eye—her heart, were all with Brandomann: she shrieked aloud. "He will not reach it ere it touches the Kraken," she cried, "and then all help will be in vain."

"Not so, dear princess," replied Serimnor; "he acts with the power of Odin, and will save your father; and then what will not his generosity deserve?"

"My life—my love!" distractedly replied the wretched Ildegarda, totally incapable of accepting any consolation, and only alive to the danger of her father.

"Oh, Odin! save him!" she cried; "and thou, thou the nameless!—the mighty in strength—the blind invincible—preserve the faithful Brandomann!"

At this instant the Kraken sunk—the hoof of Sleipner had touched him—and Brandomann sternly approached the vessel: a band of warriors, headed by her father, prepared to oppose him, and Ildegarda beheld their bright weapons gleaming above his head.

At this sight, "Harm him not," she exclaimed; "ye know not whom ye strike!"

But the next instant shewed her the folly of her fear and the mighty power of her lover. Heedless of the flashing swords, Sleipner sprung among the warriors, whose arms were now useless in their deadened hands, and Brandomann stood upon the deck, sternly reproving their presumption, and commanding the gallant ship to return home to Denmark. The vessel obeyed—the warriors knew the eight-legged steed of Odin, and were silent; but Haquin accused aloud the murderer of his daughter, for he judged he beheld the lord of the Maelstrom.

"Thy daughter lives," replied the terrible Brandomann; "but she is mine: at her entreaty I have saved thy forfeit life—but approach no more the island forbidden by Odin to mortal foot, else will I resign thee to the fate thy presumption will incur, and which, but for thy daughter's tears, thou wouldest ere now have tasted. Hence, Haquin, and learn submission!"

Sleipner plunged into the waters, and the vessel, now removed beyond the power of the whirlpool, sailed back to Denmark, while Brandomann returned to Ildegarda, by whom he was received with a welcome far surpassing his hopes or expectations. He said nothing, however, of the important service he had just rendered her; and this delicate conduct, which did not pass unobserved by the princess, created for him an advocate in her bosom stronger than his own entreaties, or those of all his friends united, could have done. She saw how tenderly Brandomann loved her, but she saw also that he was resolved not to give her pain; and, to say the truth, she could not help being pleased by this circumstance: for her gratitude, great as it certainly was, was yet not sufficiently powerful to make so cruel a sacrifice to his happiness. By the time he had landed, the storm had passed from the face of heaven, and all was as calm upon the bosom of the waters as if the fiends of Niftheim had not been raging within it but a few moments before; the party returned to sup in the palace, and all things went on as pleasingly as usual. Days, weeks, passed away, but Ildegarda, no longer wretched in submitting to the sentence she had once thought so cruel, took little heed of time, except to notice the first day of the month, which presented to her anxious eyes the person and occupations of her father. Twice, successively, she had seen him in his tent, surrounded by heroes, amid preparations for war; he was cheerful, and appeared to be encouraging the spirits of a young man, whom Ildegarda knew to be Prince Harold, and who, with a gentle, downcast look, was listening to his observations: this was confirmed to her by the accounts of Brandomann, whose cares to lighten her anxieties and anticipate her wishes sensibly affected the generous daughter of Haquin. She took increased delight in his conversation; and he, from whose presence she was at first so anxious to fly, was now frequently summoned to relieve solitude by his cheering conversation. She was herself surprised at the change; and could she have shut from her bosom the thought of her early and beautiful love, Brandomann, even in person, would not have been disgusting. As it was, he daily grew less odious, and daily grew the princess more contented with her lot; the happy society of the marble palace met nightly, and mirth, and song, and tale, gave wings to the cheerful hours.

THE RETURN

"Wilt thou begone?"
SHAKESPEARE

*O*ne night when the conversation particularly turned upon the exploits of the ancestors of Ildegarda, Sleipner, who possessed a natural love of noble actions, inquired of the boar whether King Uffon was constant in his attendance upon the nightly festival of the hall of Odin?

"He is so, frequently," replied Serimnor; "but he takes more delight in the combat of the morning—from that he is never absent—but what an extraordinary history is his!" continued the boar; "it is necessary that he should be in Asgard, for its inhabitants to believe it."

Ildegarda's attention was aroused; she had never heard of her ancestor, and she entreated Brandomann to indulge her curiosity. He took up his harp immediately—for he appeared to have no occupation so delightful as to obey her slightest wish—and thus related to her the legend of Uffon the Merciful:—

LEGEND OF UFFON
I.

There was a halo round
The golden crown which shone on Vermund's brow,
The light of many noble deeds—
Some deathless flowers
From heaven's immortal tree,
(The abode of changeless destiny),
Were wreathed
Around his conquering sword:
But years rolled on, and age
Silvered his golden locks—
And then a darkness fell
Heavily on him,
Veiling the beauty of his later day—
For Loki in hate,
Or envy, breathed on him a withering curse—
And he grew blind!
He was a childless man,
And to the gods he prayed
That his own royal diadem might fall
Upon a kindred brow.
He asked a son—
And Odin granted to his agony
The son he craved.
Again the evil one
Blighted the bud of joy—
He laid his dark hand on the infant's head,
And left its evil shadow on his brain—
He grew an idiot boy!
The Saxon king,
A wild, fierce warrior, heard of Vermund's grief,
And he did rage to snatch, with greedy hand,

The sceptre of the blind.
Madly he poured
His thousands o'er the land;
The red steel clashed—
The curling fire ran—
The ravens fed
On beauty, and the eagles gorged on strength.
The blind prince trembling heard
His people's dying groan!
The Saxon king
Rode, like the thunderbolt, his mighty steed
To the sad Danish camp.
He mocked the king—
And to his peers, with haughty action, said,
"Doth it become
The noble sons of Odin thus to bend
The knee before a blind man, and a fool?"
"Out on thee, wretch!"
The sightless prince exclaimed;
"It more becomes the warrior to protect
Than scorn the weak and aged!—
Mighty!—to thee—
Thee! whom we fear to name—
Thee! strongest pillar of great Odin's throne—
Thee! dark, but terrible!—whose woe I bear—
Thee! whose most awful name
The reckless echo dares not repeat, and we
Shudder as we pronounce!
HODER!—I call on thee!—
Be thou the judge
Between this wretch and me!"
The Saxon heard
And shrunk at that dread name—
The nobles groaned—

The father wept, and clasped,
To his chilled heart, his dumb and idiot boy.
When, lo! a wonder!—
His sacred tears fell on the youthful brow
Like holy rain upon the scorched-up earth,
And upward to the sun of glory sprung
The buried seeds of intellect—
He spoke!—
"Ha! scoffer!" said the boy, "didst thou not know
The blind and weak are sacred?"—
His eye shone
With a miraculous light—
"Hark! Saxon churl!
I summon thee unto the field of death—
I, the dumb idiot—I will meet thee there,
And on thy craven bosom write a truth,
That Vermund hath a son—Denmark a prince,
Who will protect their glories!"
The day came—
And Uffon's fiery chariot bore him forth
Unto the battle field—
Less bright—less beautiful
Is Balder when, from Lidscialf's diamond steps,
He rises to illuminate the worlds
Which wheel caressingly around him—and
Gallantly rode the Saxon.
But the king—
The blind—the father—where is he? He sits
On yonder rock, high o'er the foaming sea,
There to await the battle.
Should he fall—
His own—his only one—
Ocean will catch his form,
And hide his griefs forever.

It was a deadly fight
Between the Saxon and the Dane;
And once
There was a scream, as if the inspired boy
Was lost, for he had sunk upon his knee—
But he beheld his father's sightless eye
Upturned in agony—
And he arose—and then
Another sound was heard—a mighty shout—
The scorner of the blind was slain!
The son—he flew,
A bounding reindeer, to his father's arms—
He paused—
They were upraised,
In attitude of thankfulness;
His lips
Were pale, and still, and smiling—
But—his heart
Had broken in that fierce struggle—
He was gone—
Heimdaller's wings were shadowing him, as o'er
The wondrous bridge he trod;
Valkyries bore
His spirit to the foot of Odin's throne,
To tell of Uffon's glory.
Nameless one!
This justice was thy deed—
We worship thee,
Although we love thee not!

"No, TRULY," said Serimnor, on the conclusion of the legend, "that would be quite impossible either for heaven or earth: but glory to the good Uffon—few warriors in Valhalla are more esteemed than he. The skull of the impious Saxon is now his drinking cup; and his father, restored to sight, beholds the pledge of victory with undying felicity: and, in the combats and martial sports of the morning, the battle between his noble son and the Saxon is daily renewed, to gladden him with the sound of conquest and triumph over his shadowy foe."

"Look, Serimnor," said the horse of Odin, interrupting him impatiently, as a bright flash of lightning darted into the hall and played against his head for a moment; "Look, we are again outstaying our time—the son of Rinda is shooting his brilliant arrows, and one has already touched you: let us obey the summons, and not provoke him to make his fatal shafts unerring."

"Away, then!" cried Heidruna. The ravens flapped their wings—Brandomann rose—and the hall was cleared in a moment.

Ildegarda had hitherto been happy in the reports of the magic mirror, and satisfied with its assurances of her father's safety. On the first of the tenth month of her residence on the island, she again withdrew the curtain—but a different spectacle awaited her; Haquin was lying wounded upon his couch, pale and insensible, while his attendants were anxiously endeavouring to stanch the blood which flowed from his injured side. The princess became wild with apprehension; instantly she sought her faithful Brandomann, to pour into his bosom the grief which distracted hers. He listened with tender sympathy.

"There has been a battle between your father and Frotho, no doubt," he replied; "but though I am not informed of all the particulars, I know that Haquin will not die of this wound: take comfort from this assurance, for when did I ever deceive you?"

But Ildegarda refused all consolation, and persisted in thinking and making herself the most miserable of all human beings. Her father was ill—wounded—in need of her assistance —and she herself uncertain of his fate for a whole month at least. Her anxiety hourly increased, and her grief, too powerful to be concealed from Brandomann, affected him no less painfully than herself. It was in vain he exerted his talents to divert her anguish; she was grateful for his kindness, but did not shed one tear the less: his conversation had lost its charms, his tales and songs their interest. Brandomann discovered this, and, after a terrible struggle, his generous nature overmastered every selfish and interested feeling.

"I cannot," said he at length to the weeping princess; "I cannot bear to witness your sorrow, and know that I am the cause. For your sake I will again disobey the command of Odin, which had decreed your captivity to be perpetual; you shall go to your father: promise me that you will return hither, and you shall be swiftly conveyed to his tent—and remain with him seven days; at the close of that period you must return, or my life will pay the forfeit of my fault, and be demanded to appease the anger of Odin. Go, then, beloved princess—but sometimes think of Brandomann, and what he will suffer for your sake."

The princess could scarcely believe what she heard: in a rapture of joy she accepted the offer, and was most fervent in her promises to return at the expiration of the seven days. Brandomann sighed heavily, but made no reply to her frequent protestations of their soon meeting again.

"You shall be with your father tomorrow morning," said he: "merely take this ring—put it upon your finger when you go to rest tonight, and do the same thing when you wish to return to me; but do not wear it at any other time."

The princess joyfully accepted the gift—took an affectionate leave of her admired monster—and retired to rest full of hope and expectation—expectations which were fully realized on her awaking in the morning; for she found her couch in her father's tent, and he himself gazing upon her with tender anxiety and wonder.

The joy of Haquin, at again folding his beloved child to his bosom, was considerably damped by the narrative of her adventures, and the promise which she had given to Brandomann to return. As he did not deem it possible that she intended to keep her word, he was not a little astonished at her declaration, when she assured him she could remain with him only during the seven days. He argued strongly against her intention; and she at present, unwilling to distress him, ceased to oppose his opinions, and occupied herself entirely with the care of his health, knowing that it would always be in her power to return whenever she felt the inclination. Her tender attention was fully appreciated by Haquin, but she herself was far from being at ease in the midst of a tumultuous camp, where her wishes were not anticipated with the swift and delighted obedience of her island attendants: she had no change of dress either; a circumstance peculiarly vexatious, as she was daily surrounded by admiring warriors, who constantly paid homage to her charms —and among whom Prince Harold was not the least fervent in his expressions of devotion to her beauty. Awakening one morning after many regrets upon this subject to herself overnight, she was surprised to see the chest which ornamented her chamber at Moskoe, and which contained her superb wardrobe, standing by the side of her couch, she opened it hastily:

"Kind, generous Brandomann, always alike solicitous for my happiness and pleasure," she exclaimed; "how much do I not owe thee!"

She immediately decorated her lovely person and returned to her father, who, cheered by her presence and renovated by her care, was quickly recovering from the effects of his wound: he now informed her that Haldane was universally said to have been murdered by his uncle; and that, in consequence of their disgust at this act of cruelty, many noble Danes had resorted to the standard of Harold, whom they had unanimously called to the throne, though they held not the gentle boy in the same estimation as his more valiant brother. To this he added, that as the

young king had declared a passion for Ildegarda, he had determined to unite them despite of the wrath of Frotho, and thus
repay her long captivity by placing her upon a throne. His
daughter had many objections to this arrangement, but her
father's heart appeared to joy so deeply in its contemplation
that Ildegarda had not the courage to undeceive him: the
tenderness of Haquin, the novelty of again seeing human faces,
and the pleasure of listening to the gallant praises of the noble
Danes, at length rendered Ildegarda forgetful of her promise,
and not only seven days, but twice that number slipped away,
ere she called to mind the probable anxiety of Brandomann. She
now determined to repair her fault and hasten back to the
island, but when, upon retiring to rest, she sought her ring to
place it upon her finger, the talisman was nowhere to be found.
In great distress she hastened to her father, expecting him
perhaps to sympathize in her misfortune, but, unlike the gentle
monster of the Maelstrom, he laughed at her anxiety, and
congratulated her upon her loss; he bade her be under no
apprehension respecting her ring, since it was safe in his possession—he had stolen it on being informed of its virtue, in order
to secure her company—"which," he continued, "it appears,
without this precaution I should have lost."

He observed that he could not permit such a preposterous
union between beauty and a beast, who, instead of being a
descendant of Odin, was doubtless a member of the infernal
royal family of Lok, and consequently some diabolical sorcerer,
who had thus bought her, body and soul, of Frotho: he would
give her, he remarked, a husband better suited to her rank and
beauty, and commanded her to prepare to espouse her royal
cousin Harold, within at least ten days. Ildegarda was much
startled by this conversation; and she who in the desolate island
had mourned over the idea of perpetual captivity, now wept
with more bitterness her recovered liberty, and the prospect of
never more returning to her prison; she thought of the tender

obedience of Brandomann to her lightest wish, and his generous self-denial upon all occasions respecting her. She lamented the kind-hearted Serimnor, the chivalrous horse, the affectionate goat, and even the ravens and reindeer received the tribute of her tears; but the idea of the probable suffering of Brandomann for his devotion to her, and disobedience in her favour, filled her heart with the most poignant regret; she hated Harold, and she esteemed her Maelstrom friend, and not a day passed without the severest search for the ring that was to convey her back to his territories. At length Rinda, in pity, heard her prayers. In her father's bosom, during his sleep, she found her glittering ring, which she hastily secured as her dearest treasure, and instantly retired to rest; and when morning again looked upon her, it was in her chamber of the desolate isle.

Ildegarda scarce waited fully to throw off the fetters of sleep ere she descended to the marble hall, and instantly gave the signal which used to summon Brandomann to her presence, and which he had never neglected; now it was unheeded. Alarmed, she repeated it more strongly—Brandomann replied not to the call; half-distracted she hurried through the palace, and harrowed her own feelings by recalling to mind his mournful prediction of the fate which awaited him, should she exceed her allotted time. She shuddered to reflect how long that time had elapsed. From the palace she traversed the gardens, running wildly with an aching heart and burning brow to every quarter, and asking every object she met for tidings of her lamented Brandomann: the birds and the echoes alone replied to her mournful queries, and disconsolate and despairing she threw herself upon the sod to give vent to the bitterness of her sorrow, and lament undisturbed her affliction.

"Brandomann!" she exclaimed; "Brandomann! where art thou? friend of my soul, art thou yet in existence, or hath my ingratitude destroyed thee? Oh, if thou hearest, if thou beholdest these tears, have pity on thy wretched Ildegarda, and hasten to relieve her agony, and pardon her involuntary crime."

She started up in a sudden ecstasy, for a low groan at no great distance from her seemed to be an answer to her question; she rushed forward in that direction, and soon beheld the hapless Brandomann stretched upon the earth, and apparently in the agonies of death; but her beloved voice, the touch of her gentle hand, the glance of her worshipped eye, either of these would have recalled him to life, and now all were lavishly employed to restore him: he looked up for a moment.

Mournfully he said, "Beloved, thou art come to see me die!" and then relapsed into stupor and forgetfulness. Ildegarda wept in agony—she was hanging over him in listless sorrow, when her thoughts were aroused by the appearance of Heidruna.

"Brandomann is dying," said the white goat, "and from grief at your neglect; but you have returned, and, in compassion to your sufferings, I am permitted to restore him to you: take the bowl you see yonder, draw forth a portion of my milk, and give it to his lips; the hydromel of heaven will call him back to life."

Ildegarda obeyed—she gave the miraculous draught to Brandomann, who as instantly recovered his reason and his strength; with tears of joy she expressed her gratitude to Heidruna; and the Moskoe chief observing her delight, and too happy once more to behold her, readily forgave her all he had suffered in her absence. There was much happiness that night in the marble palace; Sleipner bowed down his arched neck to receive a pat from her snowy hand; Serimnor grinned till his huge tusks were completely visible; the ravens presented her the tips of their wings, and flew screaming about, as if *they* had been drinking the hydromel of Valhalla. Ildegarda was happy, and Brandomann dared not trust his feelings to words. Sunny walks and moonlight musings were now the pursuits of the imprisoned pair; for instead of retiring to rest, as formerly, when the Valhalla people went to their party, they roamed over the island, contemplating the stars, and talking tenderly of course, for when were love and moonshine separated? It is true, in this instance, the tenderness was all on one side; for though Ildegarda permitted it, since she saw the happiness it gave to Brandomann, she yet could not prevail upon herself to return it, or say the words he wished to hear from her lips. One evening, as thus, in the tranquil moonlight, they sat alone in the summery isle, Ildegarda was astonished, by the appearance of a wonder she had never yet remarked in the island; the moon was suddenly eclipsed by a light so glorious, yet so soft, that every object around her was visible in the brightness of beaming gold, yet without giving pain to the sense. Brandomann remarked her admiration.

"This beauteous light," said he, "is a mark of the approbation of the father of the gods, at some virtuous action of a favourite of heaven; it is Odin's fire, dear Ildegarda, the light of his glorious smile; and shining now as it does upon thee, and our lonely isle, it comes to tell thee he is satisfied with thy past conduct, and approves thy present."

Scarcely was this explanation given, ere the beauteous light died away from the mountains and the palace, and night wore again her solemn robe of darkness. As they prepared to return, the star-studded sky, the jewel-paved floor of the palaces of Asgard, sparkling with its unnumbered lights, and shining in its soft blue glory, struck on their souls with delight; and, while they were gazing in rapture, a large and brilliant star shot from its place in the heaven and vanished rapidly from their sight.

"Some noble warrior or virtuous sage has closed his eyes upon this mortal scene," said Brandomann, tenderly: "that was the star of his destiny; it fell from its seat in the heaven when he quitted his on the earth: this is the sign that tells to the survivors his fate, if it is fulfilled in the night; by day it is the vision of the rainbow bridge, the sacred arch that connects this earth with heaven, and over which the spirits of the just must pass."

"I have heard that it is only visible to mortal sight, when the peculiarly brave and virtuous ascend its brilliant road," said Ildegarda.

"And you have heard aright, dearest," replied Brandomann; "it is only then that the guardian spirit of the bridge, Heimdaller of the radiant brow, descends from his abode on its top to meet and welcome the traveller; then it is, that the light from his rushing wings, and the gems which compose his jeweled crown, shine so strongly on the arch, as to render it visible to mortal sight, clad in the reflected glories of its guardian's diadem."

On the morrow Brandomann relieved her anxiety, which had been awakened by the sight of the falling star, lest her father's should no more have a seat in the heavens, nor himself a name on the earth.

"A mild and gracious being hath left us," said he, "for the happier scenes of Asgard; Sevald is dead—the virtuous son of the abandoned Frotho is no more—he fell, as became his race, in the battle-field, contending against your victorious father and his kinsman Harold, against whom the tyrant rages and vows destruction, as now the only rival he has to fear."

The princess was satisfied by this explanation, the more especially as the first day of the month again presented the person of her father, though surrounded by the bustle of war.

ODIN

"He hath borne all things well."

SHAKESPEARE

*W*hence is it, Brandomann," said Sleipner one evening to the Scaldre, "that among those of the heroes whose virtues and glories you are nightly celebrating, I never hear the actions of Odin; why, while thus honouring his friends, are you neglectful of the great father of our race? Surely he, from whom all inspiration flows, deserves the best, ay, and first fruits of your genius!"

"It was only because I feared my feeble strains would not do justice to the lofty subject," replied Brandomann; "the glory of the father of gods and men requires a mightier hand than mine to celebrate it; Brage alone should strike the golden chord to his honour—alone should sing of deeds beyond the feeble thought of mortality; that which I can, I will; I dare not wake the voice of song, but I will speak of his wondrous deeds, that tonight, in Valhalla, thou mayest tell bright Asgard's king that I have instructed this lovely maiden what honours and love are due to the first of her race, and the friend of her father. Will it please thee, Ildegarda, to listen to the legend of Sigge?"

"Beyond all other things," replied the princess, pleasedly: and Brandomann, smiling, began—

THE LEGEND OF SIGGE.

From his high and everlasting throne in Valhalla, had Odin, the dispenser of good, poured forth, with unsparing hand, innumerable benefits upon his attendant spirits. In the burning benevolence of his heart he forgot, or he disregarded, that to some essence's obligation is pain, and gratitude a toil; so high did he raise some of those bright creations that stood nearest to his throne, that they became too great for obedience, and impatient of the most gentle restraint. Loki, the most glorious of these glorious things, seated on the lowest step of the throne of light, saw but one between him and the highest; and once on that, what should restrain him from the throne of the universe? Thus he thought, and thus he did: by his eloquence he seduced the higher spirits from their duty—by his beauty and promises the lower. The worlds of Asgard sent their governing spirits forth to fight under his banner, and Surter brought myriads to his side. For the first time since the creation, the standards of revolt flew in the cities of Asgard, and the proud Loki drove back, with contempt, the interceding ministers of Odin, who came to remonstrate upon his madness. Confident in his power, the giant spirit entered Valasciolf, the city of the king, and dared even advance to Valhalla: the immortal beings who surround the diamond throne shuddered at his presumption, and, veiling their bright heads from the terrible glances of Odin, wept the approaching destiny of companions once so beloved, which they read in the eye of their master: the sovereign of the universe gave no command to his people—he uttered no reproach—he suffered his faithful spirits to fly before the sword of Loki and the devouring fires of Surter—he even permitted the lost ones to approach the steps of his eternal throne—then, when with proud exultation they advanced to seize upon him whose power they believed departed, he calmly arose from his seat and stretched out his right hand, armed with its invincible falchion, towards his enemies; at that tremendous signal Niord let loose the oceans of heaven, and, in terrific grandeur, they came rolling down upon the revolted; the winds from all the worlds were summoned up to heaven to aid their master, and rend and scatter his offenders. Balder deserted his throne in the orb of day—and the mad and governless globe flew up into Asgard, and burst its destructive flames upon the rebels. Thor, the first-born of Odin, threw bye his star-formed diadem, girded his brow with the thunder, and, wielding the red bolt of vengeance, rushed upon them. The sightless horror rose in his terrible strength, and the arrows of Vile, unerring as the lance of Hela, flew among the foes; all was confusion, terror, and despair —cries of anguish polluted the happy city—till Odin recalled his warriors, and plunged their enemies in the burning lake, bidding the proud LokI and the ambitious Surter obtain their wish and seat themselves on thrones.

But though the power of the infernal spirits was thus curbed, it was not destroyed; and, still invincible in malice, they resolved to wound Odin through his favourite, man. Loki gave birth to the snaky sin, whose folds encircle the earth, and bade him breathe from his poisonous jaws upon her surface the blast of contention and hate: he obeyed; and man, no longer benefi-cent and kind, rose up against his brother; with bitter words, he poured curses on the father who called him into life, and smote on the bosom that had nourished him in helplessness. The father of evil beheld and smiled—his work was half accom-plished—and he called into existence death, to finish the deeds begun: the pale shadow stalked over the earth and drank the crimson blood till she grew wanton in her mirth, and besought her father for a companion: he heard, and sent Fenris up to follow her steps, and exult in her multiplied victims. The fiends in hell heard the sounds of their triumph, and shouted responsive, when the shivering spirits of the slain were hurled weeping into Niftheim. At length their cruel joy was heard in Asgard, at the same moment that sounds of sorrow ascended from the earth, from the few who still remembered his name. It was from Scythia the plaining voice arose, and the monarch, looking down from his throne, beheld the last remnant of his people sinking beneath the power of the Roman. Now then he determined to descend to the earth, not only to lead them to conquest, but to teach them wisdom and virtue. Freya, the mother of the gods, resolved to partake the toils of her husband; and Thor, the eldest born of Odin, the ruler of the air, forsook his palace of nine hundred and forty halls, laid by his terrific thunderbolt, and his diadem of twelve stars, and, debasing his giant frame to the standard of humanity, descended with his father to the earth. Cased in the armor of Scythians, they joined the troops of that beloved people, and the father god bidding them contend no longer against the power of the Roman, to whom Odin had given their country, promised to lead them to other fields, and give them other lands for their inheritance. The fierce Scythians yielded to the persuasive voice of him whom they only knew as the warrior Sigge, and, rather than submit to the slavery they abhorred, they forsook the tombs of their fathers, and sought an empire in the north.

In vain the inhabitants of these regions sought to oppose the establishment of the heaven-conducted Scythians; in every battle they were defeated and driven with loss from their cities: the arrows of Freya carried destruction to the enemy—the mallet of Thor crushed thousands—and Odin, raging through their ranks, now as a warrior, now as a ferocious lion, spread devastation through their armies, and drove them from the field. The Scythians saw these wonders; and secretly acknowledged Valhalla's lord beneath the form of Sigge. When the rage of battle was past, he lulled the wounded to repose, and arrested the parting spirits of the dying with the celestial strains of his harp; the wounds of his people were cured, and their strength restored by his celestial power, while, from the same cause, his enemies were bereft of courage and of vigor. Sweden and Norway yielded to the matchless warrior, and received with joy the unknown Sigge for their king, but the Danes refused to acknowledge the leader of armies; and Mimer, their prince, an enchanter, and the friend of Loki, opposed himself against the victorious Prince of Scythia. Before the assembled Danes he contended with the stranger in eloquence and poetry, and in these his own people were compelled, by the severe laws of truth, to yield the palm to his rival. Mimer was wise, eloquent, and brave; the strains of his harp were only inferior to those of Sigge, and he felt deeply the injury which he had sustained by the decision against him. Determined to recover, with his sword, the glory he had lost, he called his armies together, and bade defiance to the Scythians: the opposing bands drew near; furious was the contest, for now, like a tiger sprung Mimer on his foes—now as a fiery serpent stung their hearts, or crushed them in his mighty folds. As terrible raged Odin in various forms, carrying dismay around him, and thinning the ranks of the valiant Danes. At length the monarchs met—in human form stood Mimer—in human form, prepared to oppose him, stood Valhalla's mighty king: but momentary was the contest, the terrible blow of the Scythian brought the head of the Dane to his feet, as its faltering tongue pronounced the name of Odin. The foe fled to the camp, while the father of men again raised to life his beloved Scythians who had fallen in this, the greatest of his fields. At length, wishing to give peace to the weary land, he summoned the Danish chiefs to meet him in conference. Seated on a throne, he received the warriors: in one hand he held the sceptre of his power, the other rested on a golden dish, in which, now richly embalmed, and adorned with a crown of gold, lay the head of the wretched Mimer. The chiefs gazed in silence—a silence unbroken by human sounds, but disturbed by the voice of the dead, for the ghastly head opened its closed lips, fixed its eyes, and bade, in hollow but authoritative tones, its countrymen no longer oppose the will of the gods, but receive for their prince and lawgiver him who was master of the world! Again it sunk into silence, and the astonished Danes, obeying its dictates, fell at the feet of the conqueror of Mimer. And now, seated in peace on the thrones of the north, more brightly shone the unmatched virtues of Sigge. He taught his subjects husbandry—he taught them to plough the waters—he opened to them the riches of commerce—and he dug from the earth the treasures which ages had concealed in her bosom—he punished vice with severity—he rewarded virtue with munificence—he taught them letters—instructed them in the mysteries of the Runic—and obliged them to cultivate the milder graces of music and verse—he allured men to obey by the charms of his eloquence and the splendour of his glory; and he spoke to their reason by his divine Hovamaal, which he gave them as his best gift—his richest legacy. In this he bade them do no wrong to each other—to honour the eternal gods—and to render up life at the command of their country. When he beheld the good effect of his regulations, and saw his people firmly attached to his laws, he called around him his children, born of his mortal wives, of the daughters of Scythia, and, dividing his dominions among them, taught them to govern according to his ordinances and example. Satisfied with his work, he called Freya and Thor to his side, and, blessing once more his mortal children, ascended with them into the regions of light. Then loudly the Danes acknowledged Odin, and paid their homage to his glory; to his race they have ever been faithful, for they still fill the earthly thrones of their father, who, from his abode in Asgard, looks down upon his children, and crowns their lives with prosperity: and thus shall he do till the long night which is to witness the last battle of the gods—the last attack of Loki and his allies, and which for ages they have been preparing—against Odin and the happy spirits of Asgard. In the dreadful conflict, men and demons, oceans, earths, Niftheim, nay, even Asgard itself, shall be involved in one general wreck—one entire and undistinguished ruin; the infernal spirits shall fall in the convulsions—evil shall be no more—and from the ashes of the universe shall arise a brighter heaven—a gloomier hell, than those which have passed away. To the glorious seats of Gimle, the city of burnished gold—to its diamond-studded palaces and star-paved courts—shall the spirits of the just ascend, with Odin and his triumphant sons, to the enjoyment of one endless festival; while the cowards and wicked of the earth shall sink with their infernal allies—the revolted of heaven—into the caves of Nastronde, an abode more horrible than Niftheim—a den built up of the carcasses of snakes, and illuminated by devouring flames, where ever-enduring sorrow shall be the punishment of the lost, from which they shall have no power to escape, again to disturb the repose of the just.

Honour and praise to Freya—victory to Thor—glory to Odin, the greatest, and the best—hail to the master of gods and men!

Happily for his hearers, it was here, at length, that the merciless Brandomann terminated his long-winded history. Sleipner had for some time been his only auditor—Ildegarda had been nodding repeatedly—Heidruna fidgetily trotting backwards and forwards to the portal, watching the clouds—Serimnor had given two or three most portentous yawns—while the two ravens who did everything in concert, had tucked their heads under their wings, and gone fairly to sleep—but they all started up when the hum of his voice had ceased, and thanked the good Brandomann as sincerely as if they had been excessively delighted, for they were grateful that he had finished at last, and were besides too well bred not to be charmed with what had been done entirely for their amusement.

On the following day, during their usual rambles about the island, the princess looked so unusually depressed, and said so little in reply to the observations of her companion, that his attention, ever on the watch, was aroused by her sadness; tenderly he inquired the cause.

"I will tell you," replied Ildegarda: "when absent from you, and believing your life in danger, my only anxiety was to return; now, when that difficulty has passed away, I confess I am wretched respecting my father's feelings and conduct, when he shall discover that I have quitted him forever; neither is my own heart without a pang when I reflect that I shall see him no more. Oh that I knew what is to come!—that I could look into the future, and behold my destiny and his!"

"I know not that it is in my power altogether to fulfil your wishes," answered Brandomann; "but I can give you a glance into the future, so as to discover its general complexion, but not to enable you to read exactly the very page of destiny. That which I can, to gratify your curiosity, I will do—I will arrest for a few minutes the flight of the triune deity Time, and, by her appearance, we shall be able to judge of what is to come.—Urda, Werandi, Skulda!" continued Brandomann, raising his powerful voice to its utmost pitch, "obey the command of the lord of the Maelstrom, the mighty delegate of Odin—pause in your flight for a moment, and stand visibly before him!"

Scarcely was the peremptory order uttered, ere a light cloud was seen advancing towards them from the sea, and when it became stationary Ildegarda beheld a female form slowly and gracefully emerging from its centre; her features were indistinctly visible, and upon the floating misty robe that enveloped her figure, many changing objects were, some faintly, some powerfully, represented.

"It is Urda the Past," said Brandomann to Ildegarda; "the

events written upon her breast and brow are partially concealed by her garment of oblivion and doubt; and when this is penetrated by mortal sight, they are still seen through the mists of passion and prejudice, by which she is ever surrounded: look now upon her breast and brow—what objects do they represent to you?"

"I see a criminal," said the princess, "about to suffer the sentence of justice—the executioner is preparing to strike."

"To my view the representation is different," replied Brandomann; "I see a crowned king falling beneath the murderous swords of his rebellious subjects."

"I observe a dying parent," continued Ildegarda, "who consigns his child to a noble warrior who weeps by his couch, but presses the babe to his heart."

"I also see the dying father," said Brandomann, "but he resigns his infant to a demon in form, and worse than a demon in heart, for he instantly plunges a dagger in its throat: what else do you remark?"

"Many other objects," continued the princess, "but nothing clearly; the goddess herself is retiring slowly from my gaze, and to whom does she give place?"

"To Werandi the Present," answered Brandomann, "in her snow-white robe, with her unveiled face and open brow and eye —how clear she looks upon us!—and her garments will shew us our actions of this moment—but she retires, and Skulda the Future supplies her place; clad in a robe of darkness, she exhibits nothing to our eyes, and the veil which covers her person conceals also her face from our observation: she shall withdraw it, and her smile or frown will shadow forth your destiny."

The goddess gently withdrew her veil, and the soft enchanting smile which she beamed upon the princess banished anxiety from her bosom, and graced the departure of the triune spirit with the sweet attribute of benevolence.

A few days after the prophetic smile of the deity of Time had given such hope to the heart of Ildegarda, they were, while wandering about the gardens of the palace, astonished by the roaring of thunders which announced a distant storm: they were surprised by the sudden change from daylight to darkness, and were puzzling each other respecting its cause, when the storm died rapidly away, the clouds fell down in a gentle shower, and the rainbow-bridge stood out in faint splendour from the heavens.

"Look, dearest," said Brandomann; "the spirit of the bow has lowered his beautiful bridge—some of the lesser warriors are ascending to Valhalla—I will address the guardian of it, and bid him render the road and its passengers visible to your sight.— All hail Heimdaller of the coloured crown!" continued Brandomann, "the friend of Odin speaks to thee; beautiful spirit of the rushing wings and eyes of tender glory, let us look upon thy face, and the road which leads to thy dwelling!"

The silvery voice of the spirit answered him, giving an immediate assent to his desire, and in a moment the road and its travellers became visible to Ildegarda. Slowly, and with feeble steps, the wounded warriors dragged themselves on till they reached the summit of the bridge, when the gates of light flew open, and the spirit, in giving them his hand, bestowed upon them strength and beauty, and thus prepared them for the presence of Odin and the glories of the halls of Valhalla.

While Ildegarda with intense interest was watching the solemn procession of the dead, her eyes were suddenly dazzled by a brilliant light thrown upon the bridge, which now shone out in tenfold splendour, colouring the mountains of the island with tints of its beautiful hues. She looked up, and beheld the spirit of the bow descending, glorious in his youthful beauty; his diadem of many-coloured gems was on his lofty brow, and, in the ineffable loveliness of his sunny smile, there was a sweetness that made Ildegarda weep.

"He goes to welcome one of the greatest of mortal heroes," said Brandomann—"one of the favourites of Odin; his presence throws this glory round him, and at this moment the beings of earth, who gaze upon the bridge, behold its colours at the brightest: but see—at the foot of the arch there is one ascending to meet the spirit!—his wounds are terrible—his bosom is fearfully gored—and his steps are feeble and slow—but he has the brow and the port of a hero; as yet I know him not."

"But *I* do!" shrieked the hapless Ildegarda—"O Brandomann, I know him well!"

The lord of the Maelstrom looked up again, and painfully recognized the shadow—it was indeed her father—the pale inhabitant of another world, whom she saw ascending slowly to meet the welcome smile of the angel of light, was once the noble Haquin, the last friend of Harold and his sons. Brandomann gazed in grief and terror, and the sorrow he felt for the death of the warrior was scarcely mitigated by the change wrought in his wearied frame by the touch of the radiant Heimdaller.

"Ildegarda!" he cried in a voice of tenderness and pity; "Ildegarda, think not that thou art alone in the world, or that all that loved thee have left it; look up, my dear one!—look on the happiness of thy noble father, and cease to regret his fate; what could thy love offer him in exchange for this?"

Ildegarda mournfully assented as she saw his glory, and her grief became more resigned and gentle. She returned to the palace with Brandomann, who, far from attempting to console, wept with her the loss she had sustained. In the evening her friends did not as usual visit the island, but they explained the cause of their absence on the next. It was in honour of Haquin they had been detained at Valhalla, as Odin had commanded the feast earlier, in order to compliment this noble warrior—

"who now," continued Sleipner, "sits highest in the hall, and nearest to Odin's self."

Time reconciled the princess to her father's death, and to her hopeless imprisonment in Moskoe. The generous Brandomann, now that she had lost in the world all that was dear to her, and was most entirely in his power, never spoke to her of the love which it was but too plain he bore her. She saw and rewarded his virtue.

"Brandomann!" she said to him one day as they wandered through the gardens of the desolate isle; "Brandomann, friend of my heart, in the world, where my father walks no longer, I have no interest, and can never wish to return; yet I feel that I could love and render some deserving being more happy than a lonely destiny could make him; thou alone art worthy of this heart, and of the duty which I will pay thee; I cannot love thee as I once loved Haldane—as I fear I should love him still—that feeling it is not in thy power to inspire; but I honour thy virtue, and am grateful for its exercise. Wilt thou accept this hand—this heart? If so, take me, Brandomann, for I am thine!"

She threw herself, as she spoke, into the arms which opened transportedly to receive her, and bowed her head upon his breast. She could not distinguish his reply, for a sudden peal of thunder rolled above their heads, and the earth was shaken to its foundation—a frightful darkness covered the island, and shrieks and howlings rung in their ears, mingled with shouts of triumph and the cheering blasts of the trumpet. Ildegarda clung closer to her lover for protection, when a gentle, well-known voice reassured her spirits and relieved her terrors.

"Look on me, my beloved," it said; "look on me, and receive the reward of thy virtue, and the approbation of Heaven on thy choice."

The princess raised her eyes to the face of her lover, and beheld—not Brandomann, but Haldane—the one, the only beloved, the first choice of her innocent heart; it was on his bosom she leaned—it was his arm that supported her slender form: she trembled with painful emotion.

"But Brandomann?" she demanded—

"Is at thy feet, my beloved," replied the graceful warrior: "beneath that hideous form, Loki, in revenge for an ancient scorn, had condemned me to wear out my life, unless I could inspire a royal virgin with sufficient love to become my wife. Odin, in compassion to my sufferings, confined me to this island, and endowed me with sufficient power to fulfil the condition, and deceive and baffle the evil spirits themselves, by the means of their wretched agent, the detestable Frotho. Around thee stand the gallant chiefs and the Norwegian captives, who were sent against the monster of the Maelstrom, and who seemed to be destroyed by my vengeance; they are now my friends, and wait to conduct us to Denmark, where Haldane will lay his crown at thy feet."

The chiefs paid their homage to the princess, and immediately after, there arrived, to offer their sincere congratulations, her tender friends of many moons, the eight-legged, four-legged, and two-legged animals of Valhalla. Ildegarda, even on the bosom of Haldane, wept at the parting; for she knew she should behold them no more. They attended her to the shore, and beheld her embark in the gallant ship which Niord, at the command of Odin, had preserved for them in one of the ocean caves. Soon they were wafted to Denmark, and Haldane burst upon the usurper so suddenly, that he had no time even to arm his household guards for his defence. He was presiding at a festival when Haldane entered his presence; some of his nobles humbly acknowledged their prince, and the others, not caring to attack him, made the best of their way out of the palace, leaving the miserable Frotho in the power of his nephew, who, without giving him time to make his will, threw him headlong into the cistern of mead before which he was sitting.

Whether Haldane, in his natural shape, was as amiable and complaisant as he had been under his assumed one, is a question which the historian of his life cannot answer—nor whether Ildegarda, on her throne in Denmark, found as true friends and faithful servants as she had in the gulf of the Maelstrom: certain it is, she lived to a great age with her glorious husband (who was the greatest prince of the race of Dan that ever swayed the sceptre of the north), and that once or twice during their lives they had together visited the desolate isle; and the princess, to the great scandal of the ladies and gentlemen of the court, and surprise of her husband, wept bitterly on finding that the marble palace and its beautiful gardens had disappeared, the Moskoe isle had resumed its ancient appearance, and nothing remained to mark it out as the scene of such wonders as had passed in it. It has much the same character at this hour; and it would be very difficult to persuade its inhabitants, or the stranger who may visit its shores, that it once was a paradise only second to the bowers of Valasciolf's own. You, gentle reader, know better; and, complimenting you on the patience by which you have acquired this knowledge, I bid you, for the present, farewell.

NOTES TO THE LORD
OF THE MAELSTROM

Olave the Second—one of the early kings of Denmark, of the race of Dan. These princes believed themselves descended from Odin. Olave was a worthless, profligate prince, who left two sons, who succeeded him; the elder, Frotho the Fifth, murdered his brother Harold, and afterwards the assassin who, by his own order, had stabbed him. He endeavoured to secure the persons of the princes his nephews; but a nobleman, friend to their father, conveyed them out of his reach, and concealed them in a cave till they were of an age to revenge these injuries.

Asgard—the country of the gods; the Olympus of the north.

Valasciolf—its chief city, in which the principal divinities and more illustrious dead resided in magnificent palaces.

Valhalla—the chief palace of Valasciolf, the regal residence of Odin.

Niftheim—Hell. A territory of devouring flames, typifying

eternal remorse; the abode of the evil principle and his attendant spirits.

Feggo—the brother of Harwendil, King of Jutland, and uncle to
Hamlet. The latter prince feigned madness after the murder of
his father, but killed Feggo at a festival. He succeeded to the
crown, which he wore with honour, till killed in battle by Viglet,
King of Denmark.

Loki—the evil principle. He gave birth to Midgard (sin), the
snake whose folds encircle the earth—Hela (death)—and the
wolf Fenris, the guardian of the gate of hell; these were the evil
progeny of Lok, begotten for the destruction of the human race.

Surter—the evil divinity of fire—the next in rank to Loki. The
Scythians represented him as a beautiful youth; the Saxons as an
old man, to whose honour they dedicated the seventh day of the
week.

Balder—son of Odin, god of eloquence and poetry, and ruler of
the sun—the Scandinavian Apollo. He was represented as a
youth with a burning wheel upon his breast; his face resembled
the sun.

Nastronde—According to the Scandinavian mythology, at the
end of the world, during a night which was to last a year, a
tremendous battle was to be fought between the good and evil
spirits, in which the former were to conquer and reign in
Gimle, a more glorious heaven than Asgard; while the wicked
were to be banished to Nastronde, a new hell, made purposely
for them.

Maelstrom, Malestrom, or *Moskoestrom*—a tremendous whirlpool
on the Norwegian coast, very dangerous, and often fatal to

navigators venturing too near it. Moskoe is an island situated in the gulf; there are also several others.

Sleipner—the warrior horse of Odin. He had four black legs and four white ones: he generally travelled through the air.

Rinda—daughter of Balder, and mother of Vile, by Odin. The favourite goddess of the Scandinavian women.

Hydrasil—the tree of heaven, standing in the garden of Odin. It was the abode of the disposer of Man's destiny.*Heidruna*—the immortal goat, whose milk was the hydromel served up nightly at the festivals of Valhalla.

Serimnor—the wild boar, whose flesh served them for food.

Hugin and *Munin*—the raven messengers of Odin.

Thor—the warrior god—the eldest son of Odin, who, in his journey over the world, defeated Midgard, and loosened his folds from the earth; he is typical of divine justice and vengeance. In the beautiful fables of the Scalds, he is represented as a stern warrior, armed with an enormous mallet, and wearing a crown of twelve stars. He lived in a palace of Valasciolf, of five hundred and forty halls, and was the ruler and wielder of the thunderbolt.

Forsete—divinity of controversy. I believe this deity is peculiar to the Scandinavians. He lived in a palace called Glitner.

Blind horror—Hoder—whose name was never pronounced by the Scythians without fear and immediate expiation—son of Odin, and born blind—the deity of strength. He was abhorred in heaven, because, from envy, he attacked Balder, threw him from his throne, and put out the sun. Odin interfered, and punished Hoder by the arrows of Vile (lightning), and afterwards restored the sun. It was thus, in their beautiful and fanciful mythology, like the Greeks, and I think no less elegantly, that the Scalds described natural, but not understood events. This story describes an eclipse of the sun, the strong and blind Hoder signifying darkness.

Lofna—goddess of reconciliation. I believe this deity is also peculiar to the Scythians; they have deified her with great propriety. Her post could not have been a sinecure in a paradise where happiness consisted in drinking and fighting.

Hiarn—his story is strictly historical. It was Eric the Third who was so maddened by music as to commit murder for no other cause.

Geysers—boiling spouting springs in Iceland: they are near to Skalholt and Hecla; they spout water to a tremendous and incredible height.

Dofrefeld—a mighty range of Norwegian mountains, intersected by rivers and cataracts.

Dolsteen—a wonderful cavern beneath the Dofrefeld mountains.

Niord—the Scandinavian Neptune.

Uffon—this story is also historical. Shakespeare, who read Danish history, borrowed the circumstance of Vermund's death for that of Gloster in *King Lear*.

Lidscialf—the throne of Odin.

Heimdaller—guardian of the bridge Bifrost, or the rainbow, by which the happy dead ascended into Asgard. He received the souls who were selected by the Valkyries, and conducted them to Odin.

Vile—god of archery; son of Odin and Rinda.

Brage—god of music and song.

Hovamaal—bible of Odin.

Odin—a wise and virtuous warrior, whose beneficence procured him, among the early Scythians, deification. As a divinity, the father of gods and men, he is the husband of Frea (the earth), and from the union of divine love and the earth, spring light, heat, the elements, the seasons, strength, and genius, typified by Balder, Thor, Frey, Hoder, and Balder again, as orator and poet. Odin, mounted upon his horse Sleipner, represents active benevolence.

DER FREISCHÜTZ;
OR, THE MAGIC BALLS

DER FREISCHÜTZ;
OR, THE MAGIC BALLS

> "Black spirits and white,
> Blue spirits and grey,
> Mingle, mingle, mingle,
> You that mingle may."
> *THE GERMAN OF A. APEL*

*L*isten, dear wife," said Bertram, the forester of Lindenhayn, to his good and faithful Anne; "listen, I beseech you, one moment. You know I have ever done my utmost to make you happy, and will still continue to do so; but this project is out of the question. I entreat you, do not encourage the girl any farther in the notion; settle the matter decidedly at once, and she will only drop a few silent tears, and then resign herself to my wishes; but by these silly delays nothing rational can be effected."

"But, dearest husband," objected the coaxing wife, "may not Catherine be as happy with William the clerk as with Robert the gamekeeper? Indeed you do not know him: he is so clever, so good, so kind—"

"But no marksman," interrupted the forester. "The situation

which I hold here has been possessed by my family for more than two hundred years, and has always descended down in a straight line from father to son. If, instead of this girl, Anne, you had brought me a boy, all would have been well; he would have had my situation, and the wench, if she had been in existence, might have chosen for her bridegroom him whom she loved best; now the thing is impossible. My son-in-law must also be my successor, and must therefore be a marksman. I shall have, in the first place, some trouble to obtain the trial for him; and in the second, if he should not succeed, truly, I shall have thrown my girl away: so a clever huntsman she shall have. But observe, if you do not like him, I do not exactly insist upon Robert: find another active clever fellow for the girl, I will resign my situation to him, and we shall pass the rest of our lives free from anxiety and happily with our children. But hush!—not another word!—I beseech you let me hear no more of the steward's clerk."

Mother Anne was silenced; she would fain have said a few more words in favour of poor William, but the forester, who was too well acquainted with the power of female persuasion, gave her no further opportunity; he took down his gun, whistled his dog, and strode away to the forest. The next moment, the fair curled head of Catherine, her face radiant with smiles, was popped in at the door—

"Is all right, dear mother?" said she.

"Alas! no, my child; do not rejoice too soon;" replied the sorrowing Anne. "Your father speaks kindly, but he has determined to give you to nobody but a huntsman; and I know he will not change his mind."

Catherine wept, and declared she would sooner die than wed any other than her own William. Her mother wept, fretted, and scolded by turns; till at length it was finally determined to make another grand attack upon the tough heart of old Bertram; and, in the midst of a deliberation respecting the manner in which this was to be affected, the rejected lover entered the apartment.

When William had heard the cause of the forester's objection—"Is that all, my Catherine," said he, pressing the weeping girl to his bosom; "then keep up your spirits, dearest, for I will myself become a forester. I am not unacquainted with woodcraft, for I was, when a boy, placed under the care of my uncle, the chief forester Finsterbuch, in order to learn it, and only at the earnest request of my uncle the steward, I exchanged the shooting-pouch for the writing-desk. Of what use," continued the lover, "would his situation and fine house be to me, if I cannot carry my Catherine there as the mistress of it? If you are not more ambitious than your mother, dearest, and William the gamekeeper will be as dear to you as William the steward, I will become a woodsman directly; for the merry life of a forester is more delightful to me than the constrained habits of the town."

"O dear, dear William," said Catherine—all the dark clouds of sorrow sweeping rapidly over her countenance, and leaving only a few drops of glittering sunny rain, sparkling in her sweet blue eyes,—"O beloved William! if you will indeed do this, all may yet be well: hasten to the forest, seek my father, and speak to him ere he has time to pass his word to Robert."

"Away," replied William, "to the forest; I will seek him out, and offer my services as gamekeeper: fear nothing, Catherine; give me a gun, and now for the huntsman's salute."

What success he had in his undertaking was soon visible to the anxious eye of Catherine, on her father's return with him from the forest.

"A clever lad, that William," said the old man; "who would have expected such a shot in a townsman? I'll speak to the steward myself tomorrow; it would be a thousand pities such a marksman should not stick to the noble huntsman craft. Ha! Ha! he will become a second Kuno. But do you know who Kuno was?" demanded he of William.

The latter replied in the negative.

"Lo you there now!" ejaculated Bertram; "I thought I had told you long since. He was my ancestor, the first who possessed this situation. He was originally a poor horse boy in the train of the knight of Wippach; but he was clever, obliging, grew a favourite, and attended his master everywhere, to tournaments and hunting parties. Once his knight accompanied the duke on a grand hunting match, at which all the nobles attended. The hounds chased a huge stag towards them, upon whose back, to their great astonishment, sat tied a human being, shrieking aloud in a most frightful manner. There existed at that period, among the feudal lords, an inhuman custom of tying unhappy wretches who incurred their displeasure (perhaps by slight transgressions against the hunting laws) upon stags, and then driving them into the forest to perish miserably by hunger, or at least to be torn to pieces by the brambles. The duke was excessively enraged at this sight, and offered immense rewards to anyone who would shoot the stag; but clogged his benefactions with death to the marksman, should his erring bullet touch the victim, whose life he was desirous to preserve, in order to ascertain the nature of his offence. Startled by the conditions, not one of the trains attempted the rescue of the poor wretch, till Kuno, pitying his fate, stepped forward and boldly offered his services. The duke having accepted them, he took his rifle, loaded it in God's name, and earnestly recommending the ball to all the saints and angels in heaven, fired steadily into the bush in which he believed the stag had taken refuge. His aim was true; the animal instantly sprung out, plunged to the earth, and expired; but the poor culprit escaped unhurt, except that his hands and face were miserably torn by the briers. The duke kept his word well, and gave to Kuno and his descendants forever this situation of forester. But envy naturally follows merit, and my good ancestor was not long in making the discovery. There were many of the duke's people who had an eye to this situation, either for themselves or some cousin or dear friend, and these persuaded their masters that Kuno's wonderful success was entirely owing to sorcery; upon which, though they could not turn him out of his post, they obtained an order that every one of his descendants should undergo a trial of his skill before he could be accepted; but which, however, the chief forester of the district, before whom the essay is made, can render as easy or difficult as he pleases. I was obliged to shoot a ring out of the beak of a wooden bird, which was swung backwards and forwards; but I did not fail, any more than my forefathers; and he who intends to succeed me, and wed my Catherine, must be at least as good a marksman."

William, who had listened very attentively, was delighted with this piece of family history; he seized the old man's hand, and joyously promised to become, under his direction, the very first of marksmen; such as even grandfather Kuno himself should have no cause to blush for.

Scarcely had fourteen happy days passed over his head, ere William was settled as gamekeeper in the forester's house; and Bertram, who became fonder of him every day, gave his formal consent to his engagement with Catherine. It was, however, agreed that their betrothment should be kept secret until the day of the marksman's trial, when the forester expected to give a greater degree of splendour to his family festival by the presence of the duke's commissary. The bridegroom swam in an ocean of delight, and so entirely forgot himself and the whole world in the sweet opening heaven of love, that Bertram frequently insisted, that he had not been able to hit a single mark since he had aimed so successfully at Catherine.

And so it really was. From the day of his happy betrothment, William had encountered nothing but disasters while shooting. At one time his gun missed fire; at another, when he aimed at a deer, he lodged the contents of his rifle in the trunk of a tree:

when he came home, and emptied his shooting-pouch, he found, instead of partridges, rooks, and crows, and in lieu of hares, dead cats. The forester at length grew seriously angry, and reproved him harshly for his carelessness; even Catherine began to tremble for the success of the master-shot.

William redoubled his diligence, but to no purpose; the nearer the approach of the important day, the more alarming grew his misfortunes; every shot missed. At length he was almost afraid to fire a gun, lest he should do some mischief; for he had already lamed a cow and almost killed the cowherd.

"I insist upon it," said the gamekeeper Rudolph, one evening, to the party, "I insist upon it that some wizard has bewitched William, for such things could not happen naturally; therefore let us endeavour to loosen the charm—"

"Superstitious stuff!" interrupted Bertram, angrily; "an honest woodsman should not even think of such trash. Do you forget the three things which a forester ought to have, and with which he will always be successful, in spite of sorcery? Come, to your wits, answer my query."

"That can I truly," answered Rudolph; "he should have great skill, a keen dog, and a good gun."

"Enough," said Bertram; "with these three things every charm may be loosened, or the owner of them is a dunce and no shot."

"Under favor, father Bertram," said William, "here is my gun; what have you to object against it? and as for my skill, I do not like to praise myself, but I think I am as fair a sportsman as any in the country; nevertheless, it seems as if all my balls went crooked, or as if the wind blew them away from the barrel of my gun. Only tell me what I shall do. I am willing to do anything."

"It is singular," muttered the forester, who did not know what else to say.

"Believe me, William," again began Rudolph, "it is nothing

but what I have said. Try only once: go on a Friday, at midnight, to a crossroad, and make a circle round you with the ramrod, or with a bloody sword, which must be blessed three times, in the name of Sammiel—"

"Silence!" interrupted Bertram, angrily: "know ye whose name that is? He is one of the fiend's dark legion. God protect us and every Christian from him!"

William crossed himself devoutly, and would hear nothing further, though Rudolph still maintained his opinion. He passed the night in cleaning his gun, and examining minutely every screw, resolving, at dawn of day, once more to sally forth, and try his fortune in the forest. He did so, but, alas! In vain. Mischiefs thickened round him: at ten paces distance he fired three times at a deer; twice his gun missed fire, and although it went off the third time, yet the stag bounded away unhurt into the midst of the forest. Full of vexation, he threw himself under a tree, and cursed his fate, when suddenly a rustling was heard among the bushes, and a queer-looking soldier with a wooden leg came hopping out from among them.

"Holloa! huntsman," he began, laughing at the disconsolate-looking William, "what is the matter with you? Are you in love, or is your purse empty, or has anybody charmed your gun? Come, don't look so blank; give me a pipe of tobacco, and we'll have a chat together."

William sullenly gave him what he asked, and the soldier threw himself down in the grass by the side of him. The conversation naturally turned upon woodcraft, and William related his misfortunes to him.

"Let me see your gun," said the soldier. William gave it. "It is assuredly bewitched," said he of the wooden leg, the moment he had taken it in his hand; "you will not be able to fire a single shot with it; and if they have done it according to rule, it will be the same with every gun you shall take into your hands."

William was startled; he endeavoured to raise objections

against the stranger's belief in witches, but the latter offered to give him a proof of the justice of his opinions.

"To us soldiers," said he, "there is nothing strange; and I could tell you many wonderful things, but which would detain us here till night. But look here, for instance: this is a ball which is sure of hitting its mark, because it possesses some particular virtue: try it; you won't miss."

William loaded his gun, and looked around for an object to aim at. A large bird of prey hovered high above the forest, like a moving dot;—

"Shoot that kite," said the one-legged companion. William laughed at his absurdity, for the bird was hovering at a height which the eye itself could scarcely reach.

"Laugh not, but fire," said the other, grimly; "I will lay my wooden leg that it falls."

William fired, the black dot sunk, and a huge kite fell bleeding to the ground.

"You would not be surprised at that," said he of the wooden leg to the huntsman, who was speechless and staring with astonishment; "you would not, I repeat, be surprised at that, if you were better acquainted with the wonders of your craft. Even the casting of such balls as these is one of the least important things in it; it merely requires dexterity and courage, because it must be done in the night. I will teach you for nothing when we meet again; now I must away, for the bell has tolled seven. In the meantime—here, try a few of my balls; still you look incredulous—well—till we meet again."

The soldier gave William a handful of balls, and departed. Full of astonishment, and still distrusting the evidence of his senses, the latter tried another of the balls, and again struck an almost unattainable object: he loaded his gun in the usual manner, and again missed the easiest! He darted forward to follow the crippled soldier, but the latter was no longer in the forest; and William was obliged to remain satisfied with the promise which he had given of meeting him again hereafter.

Great joy it gave to the honest forester when William returned, as before, loaded with game from the forest. He was now called upon to explain the circumstance; but not being prepared to give a reason, and above all, dreading to say anything upon the subject of his infallible balls, he attributed his ill luck to a fault in his gun, which he had only, he pretended, last night discovered and rectified.

"Did I not tell you so, wife," said Bertram, laughing. "Your demon was lodged in the barrel; and the goblin which threw down father Kuno this morning, sat grinning on the rusty nail."

"What say you of a goblin," demanded William; "and what has happened to father Kuno?"

"Simply this," replied Bertram; "his portrait fell of itself from the wall this morning, just as the bell tolled seven; and the silly woman settled it that a goblin must be at the bottom of the mischief, and that we are haunted accordingly."

"At seven," repeated William, "at seven!" and he thought, with a strange feeling of affright, of the soldier who parted from him exactly at that moment.

"Yes, seven," continued Bertram, still laughing. "I do not wonder at your surprise; it is not a usual ghostly hour, but Anne would have it so."

The latter shook her head doubtfully, and prayed that all might end well; while William shivered from head to foot, and would secretly have vowed not to use the magic balls, but that the thought of his ill luck haunted him.

"Only one of them," said he internally; "only one of them for the master-shot, and then I have done with them forever."

But the forester urged him the next instant to accompany him into the forest; and as he dared not excite fresh suspicions of his want of skill, nor offend the old man by refusing, he was again compelled to make use of his wondrous balls; and in the course of a few days he had so accustomed himself to the use of them, and so entirely reconciled his conscience to their doubtful origin, that he saw nothing sinful or even objectionable in the business. He constantly traversed the forest, in the hope of meeting the strange giver of the balls; for the handful had decreased to two, and if he wished to make sure of the master-shot, the utmost economy was necessary. One day he even refused to accompany Bertram, for the next was to be the day of trial, and the chief forester was expected: it was possible he might require other proofs than the mere formal essay, and William thus felt himself secure. But in the evening, instead of the commissary, came a messenger from the duke, with an order for a large delivery of game, and to announce that the visit of the chief forester would be postponed for eight days longer.

William felt as if he could have sunk into the bosom of the earth, as he listened to the message, and his excessive alarm would have excited strange suspicions, if all present had not been ready to ascribe it to the delay of his expected nuptials. He was now obliged to sacrifice at least one of his balls, but he solemnly swore nothing should rob him of the other but the forester's master-shot.

Bertram was outrageously angry when William returned from the forest with only one stag; for the delivery order was considerable. He was still more angry the next day at noon, when Rudolph returned loaded with an immense quantity of game, and William returned with none: he threatened to dismiss him, and retract his promise respecting Catherine, if he did not bring down at least two deer on the following day. Catherine was in the greatest consternation, and earnestly besought him to make use of his utmost skill, and not let a thought of her interrupt his duties while occupied in the forest. He departed—his heart loaded with despair. Catherine, he saw too plainly, was lost to him forever; and nothing remained but the choice of the manner in which he should destroy his happiness. Whilst he stood lost in the agonizing anticipation of his impending doom, a herd of deer approached close to him. Mechanically he felt for his last ball; it felt tremendously heavy in his hand: he was on the point of dropping it back, resolving to preserve his treasure at every hazard, when suddenly he saw —O sight of joy!—the one-legged soldier approaching. Delightedly he let the ball drop into the barrel, fired, brought down a brace of deer, and hastened forward to meet his friend; but he was gone! William could not discover him in the forest.

"Hark ye, William!" said the forester to him in the evening, rousing him from the torpor of grief into which he had fallen; "you must resent this affront as earnestly as myself: nobody shall dare utter falsehoods of our ancestor Kuno, nor accuse him as Rudolph is now doing. I insist," continued he, turning again to the latter, "if good angels helped him (which was very likely, for in the Old Testament we frequently read of instances of their protection), we ought to be grateful, and praise the wonderful goodness of God. But nobody shall accuse Kuno of practicing the black art. He died happily—ay, and holily, in his bed, surrounded by children and grandchildren—which he who carries on a correspondence with the evil one never does. I saw a terrible example of that myself, when I was a forester's boy in Bohemia."

"Let us hear how it happened, good Bertram," said all the listeners; and the forester nodded gravely, and continued.

"I shiver when I think of it; but I will tell you nevertheless. When a young man, practicing with other youths under the chief foresters, there used frequently to join us a town lad, a fine daring fellow, who, being a great lover of field sports, came out to us as often as he could. He would have made a good marksman, but was too flighty and thoughtless; so that he frequently missed his mark. Once, when we ridiculed his awkwardness, we provoked him into a rage, and he swore by all that was holy that he would soon fire with a more certain aim than any game-keeper in the country, and that no animal should escape him, either in the air or on the earth. But he kept his light oath badly. A few days afterwards an unknown huntsman roused us early, and told us that a man was lying in the road and dying without assistance. It was poor Schmid. He was covered with wounds and blood, as if he had been torn by wild beasts: he could not speak, for he was quite senseless, with scarcely any appearance of life. He was conveyed to Prague, and just before his death declared, that he had been out with an old mountain huntsman to a crossroad, in order to cast the magic balls, which are sure of hitting their mark; but that making some fault or omission, the demon had treated him so roughly that it would cost him his life."

"Did he not explain?" asked William, shuddering.

"Surely," replied the forester. "He declared before a court of justice, that he went out to the crossroad with the old game-keeper; that they made a circle with a bloody sword, and afterwards set it round with skulls and bones. The mountain hunter then gave his directions to Schmid as to what he was to do: he was to begin when the clock struck eleven to cast the balls, and neither to cast more nor fewer than sixty-three; one either above or under this number would, when the bell tolled midnight, be the cause of his destruction: neither was he to speak a single word during his work, nor move from the circle, whatever might happen, above, below, or around him. Fulfilling these conditions, sixty balls would be sure of hitting, and the remaining three only would miss. Schmid had actually begun casting the balls when, according to what we could gather from him, he saw such cruel and dreadful apparitions, that he at length shrieked and sprung out of the circle, falling senseless to the ground; from which trance he did not recover till under the hands of the physician in Prague."

"Heaven preserve us!" said the forester's wife, crossing herself.

"It is a very deadly sin undoubtedly," pursued Bertram, "and a true woodsman would scorn such practice. He needs nothing but skill, and a good gun, as you have lately experienced, William. I would not, for my own part, fire off such balls for any price; I should always fear the fiend would, at some time or other, conduct the ball to his own mark instead of to mine."

Night drew round them with the conclusion of the forester's story. *He* went to his quiet bed, but William remained in restless agony. It was in vain that he attempted to compose himself. Sleep fled entirely from his spirit. Strange objects flitted past him, and hovered like dark omens over his pillow. The strange soldier of the forest, Schmid, Catherine, the duke's commissary, all rushed before his eyes, and his fevered imagination converted them into the most dreadful groups. Now, the miserable Schmid stood warningly before him, and hollowly pointed to his newly bleeding wounds; then the dark distorted face faded to the pallid features of Catherine wrestling with the strength of death; while the wild soldier of the forest stood mocking his agony with a hellish laugh of scorn. The scene then changed to his mind, and he stood in the forest before the commissary, preparing for the master-shot. He aimed—fired—missed, Catherine sunk down on the earth. Bertram drove him away; while the one-legged soldier, now again a friend, brought him fresh balls; but too late—the trial was over, and he was lost.

In this manner wore away his agonized night, and with the earliest dawn he sought the forest, hoping to meet with the soldier; the clear morning air chased away the dark images of sleep from his brow, and ennerved his drooping spirit.

"Fool!" said he to himself, "because I cannot understand what is mysterious, must the mystery therefore be a sin? Is what I seek so contrary to nature that it requires the aid of spirits to obtain it? Does not man govern the mighty instinct of animals, and make them move according to the will of their master? Why then should he not be able, by natural means, to command the course of inanimate metal which receives force and motion only through him? Nature is rich in wonders which we do not comprehend, and shall I forfeit my happiness for an ignorant prejudice only? No! Spirits I will not call upon, but nature and her hidden powers I will challenge and use, even though unable to explain its mystery. I will seek the soldier, and, if I cannot find him, I will at least be bolder than Schmid, for I have a better cause. He was urged by presumption, I by love and honour."

But the soldier appeared not, however earnestly William sought him; neither could any of those of whom he inquired give him the slightest information respecting him, and two days were wasted in these anxious and fruitless inquiries.

"Then be it so," exclaimed the unhappy young man; and in a fit of despair he resolved to cast the magic balls in the forest.

"My days," he added, "are numbered to me; this night will I seek the crossroad. Into its silent and solitary recess no one will dare to intrude; and the terrible circle will I not leave till the fearful work shall be done."

But when the shadows of evening fell upon the earth, and after William had provided lead, bullet-mold, and coals, for his nocturnal occupation, he was gently detained by Bertram, who felt, he said, so severe an oppression, that he entreated him to remain in his chamber during the night. Catherine offered her services, but they were, to her astonishment, declined.

"At any other time," said her father, "I should have preferred you, but tonight it must be William. I shall be happier if he will remain with me."

William hesitated. He grew sick in his inmost heart. He would have objected, but Catherine's entreaties were so earnest, her voice so irresistible, that he had nothing to oppose against her wishes. He remained in the chamber, and in the morning Bertram's dark fears had faded, and he laughed at his own absurdity. He proposed going to the forest, but William, who intended to devote the day to his search for the soldier, dissuaded him, and departed alone. He went, but returned disappointed, and once more resolved to seek the forest at night. As he approached the house, Catherine met him.

"Beloved William," said she, "you have a visitor, and a dear one, but you must guess who it is."

William was not at all disposed to guess, and still less to receive visits; for at that time the dearest friend would have been the most unwelcome intruder. He answered peevishly, and was thinking of a pretext to turn back, when the door of the house opened, and the pale moon threw her soft ray upon a venerable old man, in the garb of a huntsman, who extended his arms towards him; and "William!" said a kind and well-known voice, and the next instant the young forester found himself folded to the bosom of his beloved uncle.

Ah! magic of early ties, dear recollections, and filial gratitude! William felt them all; his heart was full of joy, and all other thoughts were forgotten. Suddenly spoke the warning voice to the tranquil happy dreamer. The midnight hour struck, and William, with a shudder, remembered what he had lost.

"But one night more remains to me," said he; "tomorrow, or never."

His violent agony did not escape the eye of his uncle, but he ascribed it to fatigue, and excused himself for detaining him from his needful rest, on account of his own departure, which he could not delay beyond the following day.

"Yet grieve not, William," said the old man as he retired to rest; "grieve not for this short hour thus spent, you will only sleep the sounder for it."

William shivered, for to his ear these words conveyed a deeper meaning. There was a dark foreboding in his heart, that the execution of his plan would forever banish the quiet of sleep from his soul.

But day dawned—passed—and evening descended.

"It must be now or never," thought William, "for tomorrow will be the day of trial."

The females had been busied in preparations for the wedding and the reception of their distinguished guest. Anne embraced William when he returned, and, for the first time, saluted him with the dear name of son. The tender joy of a young and happy bride glittered in the sweet eyes of Catherine. The supper-table was covered with flowers, good food, and large bottles of long-hoarded wine from the stores of Bertram.

"Children," said the old man, "this is our own festival; let us, therefore, be happy: tomorrow we shall not be alone, though you may, perhaps, be happier. I have invited the priest, dear William, and when the trial is over—"

A loud shriek from Catherine interrupted the forester. Kuno's picture had again fallen from its place, and had struck her severely on the forehead. Bertram grew angry.

"I cannot conceive," said he, "why this picture is not hung properly; this is the second time it has given us a fright: are you hurt, Catherine?"

"It is of no consequence," replied the maiden, gently wiping away the blood from her bright curls; "I am less hurt than frightened."

William grew sick when he beheld her pale face, and forehead bathed in blood. So he had seen her in his distempered dreams on that dreadful night: and this reality conjured up all those fearful fantasies anew. His determination of proceeding in his plan was shaken; but the wine, which he drank in greater quantities than usual, filled him with a wild courage, and innerved him to undertake its execution. The clock struck nine. Love and valour must combat with danger, thought William. But he sought in vain for a decent pretense to leave his Catherine. How could he quit her on the bridal eve? Time flew with the rapidity of an arrow, and he suffered agonies even in the soft arms of rewarding love. Ten o'clock struck: the decisive moment was come. Without taking leave, William started from his bride, and left the house to range the forest.

"Whither go you, William?" said her mother, following him, alarmed.

"I have shot a deer, which I had forgotten," answered the youth.

She still entreated, and Catherine looked terrified, for she felt that there was something (though she knew not what) to fear, from his distracted manner. But their supplications were unheeded. William sprung from them both, and hastened into the forest.

The moon was on the wane, and gleamed a dark red light above the horizon. Grey clouds flew rapidly past, and sometimes darkened the surrounding country, which was soon relighted up by the wild and glittering moonlight. The birch and aspen trees nodded like spectres in the shade; and to William the silver poplar was a white shadowy figure, which solemnly waved, and beckoned him to return. He started, and felt as if the two extraordinary interpositions to his plan, and the repeated falls of the picture, were the last admonitions of his departing angel, who thus warned him against the commission of an unblessed deed. Once more he wavered in his intention. Now he had even determined to return, when a voice whispered close to him,

"Fool! hast thou not already used the magic balls, and dost thou only dread the toil of labouring for them?" He paused.

The moon shone brilliantly out from a dark cloud, and lighted up the tranquil roof of the forester's humble dwelling. William saw Catherine's window shine in the silvery ray, and he stretched out his arms towards it, and again directed his steps towards his home.

Then the voice rose whisperingly again around him, and, "Hence!—to thy work!—away!" it murmured; while a strong gust of wind brought to his ear the stroke of the second quarter.

"To my work," he repeated; "ay; it is cowardly to return half way—foolish to give up the great object, when, for a lesser, I have already perhaps risked my salvation. I will finish."

He strode rapidly forward. The wind drove the fugitive clouds over the moon, and William entered the deep darkness of the forest. Now he stood upon the crossroad; the magic circle was drawn; the skulls and bones of the dead laid in order around it; the moon buried herself deeper in the cloudy mass, and left the glimmering coals, at intervals fanned into a blaze by the fitful gusts of wind, alone to lighten the midnight deed, with a wild and melancholy glare. Remotely the third quarter sounded from a dull and heavy tower clock. William put the casting ladle upon the coals, and threw the lead into it, together with three balls, which had already hit their mark, according to the huntsman's usage; then the forest began to be in motion; the night ravens, owls, and bats, fluttered up and down, blinded by the glare of light. They fell from their boughs, and placed themselves among the bones around the circle, where, with hollow croakings and wild jabberings, they held an unintelligible conversation with the skulls. Momentarily their numbers increased, and among and above them hovered pale cloudy forms, some shaped like animals, some like human beings. The gusts of wind sported frightfully with their dusky vapory forms, scattering and reuniting them like the dews of the evening shades. One form alone stood motionless and unchanged near the circle, gazing with fixed and woeful looks at William; once it lifted up its pale hands in sorrow, and seemed to sigh. The fire burned gloomily at the moment; but a large grey owl flapped its wings, and fanned the dying embers into light. William turned shivering away; for the countenance of his dead mother gazed mournfully at him from the dark and dusky figure.

The bell tolled eleven; the pale figure vanished with a groan; the owls and night ravens flew screeching up into the air, and the skulls and bones clattered beneath their wings. William knelt down by his hearth of coals. He began steadily to cast, and, with the last sound of the bell, the first ball fell from the mold.

The owls and the skulls were quiet; but along the road an old woman, bent down with the weight of age, advanced towards the circle. She was hung round with wooden spoons, ladles, and other kitchen utensils, which made a frightful clattering. The owls screeched at her approach, and caressed her with their wings. Arrived at the circle, she stooped down to seize the bones and the skulls; but the coals hissed flames at her, and she drew back her withered hands from the fire. Then she paced round the circle, and, grinning and chattering, held up her wares towards William.

"Give me the skulls," she gabbled; "give me the skulls, and I will give thee my treasures; give me the skulls, the skulls; what canst thou want with the trash? Thou art mine—mine, dear bridegroom; none can help thee: thou canst not escape me; thou must lead with me in the bridal dance. Come away, thou bridegroom mine!"

William's heart throbbed; but he remained silent, and hastened on with his work. The old woman was not a stranger to him. A mad beggar had often haunted the neighbourhood, until she found an asylum in the mad-house. Now, he knew not whether her appearance was a reality or a delusion. In a short time she grew enraged, threw down her stick, and chattered anew at William.

"Take these for our nuptial night," she cried: "the bridal bed is ready, and tomorrow, when evening cometh, thou wilt be wedded to me. Come soon, my love; delay not, my bridegroom; come soon." And she hobbled slowly away into the forest.

Suddenly there arose a rattling like the noise of wheels,

mingled with the cracking of whips and shouting of men. A carriage came headlong, with six horses and outriders.

"What is the meaning of all this in the road?" cried the foremost horseman.

"Room there!" William looked up. Fire sprung from the hoofs of the horses, and round the wheels of the carriage: it shone like the glimmering of phosphorus. He suspected a magical delusion, and remained quiet.

"On, on, upon it!—over it!—down! down!" cried the horseman; and in a moment the whole troop stormed in headlong upon the circle.

William plunged down to the earth, and the horses reared furiously above his head; but the airy cavalry whirled high in the air with the carriage, and, after turning several times round the magic circle, disappeared in a storm of wind, which tore the tops of the mightiest trees, and scattered their branches to a distance.

Some time elapsed ere William could recover from his terror. At length he compelled his trembling fingers to be steady, and cast a few balls without farther interruption. Again the well-known tower clock struck, and to him in the dreadful solitary circle, consoling as the voice of humanity, rose the sound from the habitations of men, but the clock struck the quarter thrice. He shuddered at the lightning-like flight of time; for a third part of his work was hardly done. Again the clock struck, for the fourth time!—Horror!—his strength was annihilated, every limb was palsied, and the mold fell out of his trembling hand. He listened, in the quiet resignation of despair, for the stroke of the full, the terrible, midnight hour. The sound hesitated—delayed—was silent. To palter with the awful midnight was too daring and too dangerous even to the dreadful powers of darkness. Hope again raised the sunk heart of William; he hastily drew out his watch, and beheld it pointing to the second quarter of the hour. He looked gratefully up towards heaven, and a feeling of piety moderated the transport, which, contrary to the laws of the dark world, would otherwise have burst forth in loud and joyous exclamations.

Strengthened, by the experience of the last half-hour, against any new delusion, William now went boldly on with his work. Everything was silent around him, except that the owls snored in their uneasy sleep, and at intervals struck their beaks against the bones of the dead. Suddenly it was broken by a crackling among the bushes. The sound was familiar to the sportsman, and, as he expected, a huge wild boar broke through the briers, and came foaming towards the circle. Believing this to be a reality, he sprung hastily on his feet, seized his gun, and attempted to fire. Not a single spark came from the flint. Startled at his danger, he drew his hunting knife to attack it—when the bristly savage, like the carriage and the horses, ascended high above his head, and vanished into the silent fields of air.

The anxious lover worked on steadily to regain the time he had so unhappily lost. Sixty balls were cast. He looked joyfully upwards; the clouds were dispersing, and the moon again threw her bright rays upon the surrounding country; he was rejoicing in the approaching end of his labours, when an agonized voice, in the tones of Catherine, shrieked out the name of "William!" In the next moment, he beheld his beloved dart from among the bushes, and gaze fearfully around her. Following her distracted steps, and panting closely behind her, trod the mad beggar woman, extending her withered arms towards the fugitive, whose light dress, fluttering in the wind, she repeatedly attempted to grasp. Catherine collected her expiring strength in one desperate effort to escape, when the long-sought soldier of the forest planted himself before her and delayed her flight. The hesitation of the moment gained time for the mad woman, who sprung wildly upon Catherine, and grasped her in her long and fleshless hands. William could endure it no longer, he dashed the last ball from his hand, and was on the point of springing from the circle, when the bell tolled midnight, and the delusion vanished. The owls knocked the skulls and bones cluttering against each other, and flew up again to their hiding places; the coals were suddenly extinguished; and William sunk, exhausted with fatigue, to the earth; but there was no rest for him in the forest; he was again disturbed by the slow and sullen approach of a stranger, mounted upon a huge and coal-black steed: he stopped before the demolished magic circle, and, addressing the huntsman—"You have stood the trial well," said he; "what do you require of me?"

"Of you, stranger, nothing," replied William; "of that of which I had need, I have prepared for myself."

"But with my assistance," continued the stranger; "therefore a share of it belongs to me."

"Certainly not," replied the huntsman; "I have neither hired you nor called upon you."

The horseman smiled. "You are bolder than your equals are wont to be," said he. "Take then the balls which you have cast: sixty for you, three for me. The first hit, the second missed. When we meet again you will understand me."

William turned away. "I will not meet you again; I will never see you more," he cried, trembling.

"Why do you turn from me?" demanded the stranger, with a horrible laugh: "do you know me?"

"No; no," said the huntsman, shuddering; "I know you not; I will not even look upon you. Whoever you may be, leave me."

The black horseman turned his steed. "The rising hairs of your head," cried he with gloomy gravity, "declare that you do know me. You are right; I am he whom you name in the secrecy of your soul, and shudder to think you have done so."

At these words he disappeared, and the trees under which he had stood let their withered branches sink helpless and dead to the earth.

"Merciful Heaven! William," said Catherine, on remarking

his pale and distracted look on his return after midnight; "what has happened to you? you look as if you had just risen from the grave."

"It is the night air," he replied; "and I am not well."

"But, William," said the forester, who had just entered, "why then would you go to the forest: something has happened to you there. Boy, you cannot thus blind me."

William was startled; the sad solemnity of Bertram's manner struck him. "Yes, something has occurred," said he; "but have patience for a few days, and all shall be explained to your satisfaction."

"Willingly, dear son," interrupted the forester; "question him no further, Catherine. Go to your needful rest, William, and indulge in hope of the future. He who goes on in his occupation openly and honestly, never can be harmed by the evil spirits of the night."

William had need of all his dissimulation; for the old man's observations so nearly meeting the truth, his forbearing love, and unshaken confidence in William's honesty, altogether distracted his mind: he hastened to his room, determined to destroy the magical preparation.

"But one ball—only one will I use," exclaimed he, weeping aloud, with his folded hands held up to heaven; "and surely this determination will efface the sin of the deed I have committed. With a thousand acts of penitence I will make atonement for what is past, for I cannot now step back without betraying my happiness, my honour, and my love."

And with this resolution he calmed the tumult of his spirits, and met the rays of the morning sun with more tranquility than he had dared to hope.

The commissary of the duke arrived; he proposed a shooting party in the forest, before the trial of skill took place.

"For, though we must certainly retain the old form," said he, "of the essay shot, yet the skill of the huntsman is, after all, best proved in the forest: so come, young marksman, to the woods."

William's cheek grew pale, and he earnestly tried to excuse himself from accompanying them. But, when this was refused by the chief forester, he entreated at least to be allowed to fire his trial shot before their departure. Old Bertram shook his head, doubtingly: "William," said he, "should my suspicion of yesterday be just—"

"Father!" replied the youth; and no longer daring to hesitate, he departed with them to the forest.

Bertram had in vain endeavoured to suppress his forebodings and assume a cheerful countenance. Catherine too was dejected, and it was not until the arrival of the priest that she recollected her nuptial garland: her mother had locked it up, and, in her haste to open the chest, broke the lock, and was obliged to send into the village for another wreath, as too much time had been wasted in endeavouring to recover the first.

"Let them give you the handsomest," said Anne to the little messenger, "the very handsomest they have."

The boy accordingly chose the most glittering, and the seller, who misunderstood him, gave him a death garland, composed of myrtle and rosemary, intermingled with silver. The mother and daughter beheld and recognized the mysterious intimation of fate; they embraced each other in silence, and endeavoured to smile away their terror, in imputing it to the boy's mistake. Again the broken lock was tried; it opened easily now; the wreaths were changed, and the bridal garland was twined around Catherine's brilliant locks.

The sportsmen returned from the forest. The commissary was inexhaustible on the subject of William's wondrous skill.

"It almost appears ridiculous," said he, "after such proofs, to require any further trial; yet, in honour of the old custom, we must perform what appears superfluous; we will therefore finish the business as quickly as possible. There, upon that pillar, sits a dove, shoot it."

"For God's sake," said Catherine, hastily approaching, "do not shoot that dove. Alas! in my sleep last night I was myself a dove, and my mother, while fastening a ring round my neck, on your approaching us became covered with blood."

William drew back his gun; but the chief forester smiled. "So timid, little maiden!" said he, "that will never do for a huntsman's bride: come, courage! courage!—or is the dove a favourite, perhaps?"

"Ah, no," she replied, "it is but fear."

"Well then," replied the commissary, "have courage; and now, William, fire!"

The shot fell, and, in the same moment, Catherine sunk, with a loud scream, to the earth.

"Silly girl," exclaimed the commissary, lifting her up: but a stream of blood flowed over her face, her forehead was shattered, for the ball of the rifle was lodged in the wound. William turned, on hearing loud shrieks behind him, and beheld his Catherine pale, weltering in her blood, and by her side the soldier of the forest, who, with a fiendish laugh of scorn, pointed to his dying victim, and cried aloud to William, "Sixty hit, three miss!"

"Accursed fiend!" shrieked the wretched youth, striking at the detested form with his sword, "hast thou thus deceived me?"

His agony permitted no further expression, for he sunk senseless to the earth by the side of the victim bride. The commissary and priest in vain endeavoured to console the childless heart-broken parents. The mother had scarcely laid the prophetic garland of death upon the bosom of the bridal corpse, when her sorrow and life expired with her last-shed tear: the solitary father soon followed her, and the miserable William closed his life in the mad-house.

THE RING AND THE STREAM

THE RING AND THE STREAM

Scene—A Valley in the Isle of Paros.—Time—Day.

ANDRONICUS *and* BASIL.

Andronicus. What hath inspired this happy change, my thought
Hath not divined, yet doth it sooth my soul,
And fall as dew upon my aching heart,
Soft'ning its rugged sorrows.—Since the hour
When the great King of Shadows mark'd the maid—
His beautiful betroth'd, and, in the pride
Of his omnipotent rivalship, he woo'd,
And won the virgin to his icy bed;—
Till latterly, he hath not smiled nor spoke,
But sat, a very emblem of despair—
A statue of the loveliest, but most sad.
Chisell'd by misery's hand—seem'd he, as were
The current of his anguish in its course
Frozen in his young bosom; but, at once,
A kindly sunbeam struck upon the ice,
Melted the stream, and gently bade it flow

Away from his rent bosom. He did smile,
And breath soft cadences of mournful airs,
In such enchanting melancholy mood,
That I did weep for very happiness,
Almost too much of joy; he spoke to me
Of resignation, and of sacred bliss,
Known only to the sufferer, and of joys
Not of this coarser world; and then again
He smiled and sang—and so accordant were
That smile and song, and both so breath'd of Heaven,
That, for a moment, I did think my son
Had pass'd away from earth, and that I saw
His happy wandering spirit.

Basil. This is wild—
Dreamings of Fancy, spectre-circled power—
Who holds as strong an empire o'er thy brain
As o'er the young Leontine's. I would learn
Whence comes this wondrous change. It is not well
That I, his friend, who shared in all his grief,
Should not partake his pleasures. Pray you, strive
To win the secret from him.

Andronicus. No l—for me,
It is enough that I no more behold
The stillness of despair.—Once more, he lives.—
To force into his secrets—to intrude
Into his bosom's counsels, were to break
Again the slender links of that light chain
Which binds him to mortality.—Oh, no
I cannot, and I will not pain my son
By this unhallow'd wondering—'Tis enough
That he is mine again.—Some friendly hand
Hath pour'd, perchance, soft balm upon the wound

Of his poor bleeding heart; or, kindlier Heaven
Hath, in its mercy, heal'd the bitter stripes
Its wisdom had inflicted.—He doth love,
And from his boyhood, was his soul entranced
By Nature's majesty; and now he drinks
Deeper of her intoxicating cup
Of love, and is, for his repose, become
Delirious with her beauty.—He doth roam
Nightly by hill and valley.—Near the stream
Which wanders round Marpesus' marble caves
Goes he by night, and with the silver waves,
Singing unto the pale lamp of the heaven,
He doth unite his low and mournful song;
And then, upon its bank he lieth down,
List'ning the flowers grow; and they do tell
Their secrets to his ear; for he replies,
And holds sweet converse with them.—He is now
A fair celestial thing, like those which fill
The air when it is clearest—when the gales.
Come laden with ambrosial odors, brought
From flowery beds of Paradise upon
The spirits' golden wings.—Disturb him not—
He who can treasure for himself a source
Of happiness, unsought of brother man,
Is surely wise. So, in his wisdom, let
My loved Leontine rest.

Basil. Not so, old man—
He who doth in the dungeons of his soul
His pains and pleasures thus in bondage hide,
Disdaining help and pity from mankind,
Is of mankind no longer; he hath loosed
The girdle of mortality, and stands
Without its friendly circle.—He who hath

No friends deserves them not.—Thy son hath thrown
Human compassion from him, and hath found
Peace, where man should not seek it.—Were his bliss
Thus innocent, as thou deem'st it, would it be
Veil'd from his tender father, and his friend,
By the huge marble curtains of the caves
Of high Marpesus' mountain? It is said
Thy son hath union made with that wild man
From the far distant East, who hid his crimes
From justice in those caverns. It is said,
That when some few weeks since he closed his eyes,
And yielded to the demons his dark soul,
It was on thy son's bosom, who became
His pupil and his heir, and from his lip
Received the secrets of another world,
To outrage things of this.—His wanderings
Are not alone, for he hath still been heard
In invocation loud; but 'tis decreed
This crime shall not endure, since we will spy
Upon his wand'rings; and, if he have done
That which the angels shriek at, he shall die.—
The church, the state, alike demand his life—
The sorcerer shall perish!—Look where comes
Thy Leontine.—Now rend the secret from him,
Or dread the arm of justice.

[*Exit.*]

Enter Leontine.

Leontine. How the day
Lingers upon the world!—Methinks it knows
That I would have it gone, and stays to mark
How I will curb my spirit, and resign

My will in silence, and by patience prove
My worthiness of that most precious gift
Which is my nourishment of life—my sire!
Ah, pardon me, and on this thoughtless head
Breathe a fond father's blessing.

Andronicus. Gentle son,
High Heaven's should be more valued.—I did hope
Such was thy holy thought—but there are those
Who say, thou art at war with all of good—
That Heaven's blessings are as things of nought,
And gifts of darker worlds have won thy soul
From its God-vow'd obedience.—Dearest son,
I would not give thee pain, for I rejoice
To see thee thus collected; but there are
Some who, in this most wondrous sudden change,
See much of mystery and secret sin;
And thy lone wanderings are at length become
The sad theme of the island.—Wilt thou not
Tell to thy father's ear thy source of joy?
Think'st thou *he* could betray thee?

Leontine. Oh, no, no—
But I am not permitted—should I once
Reveal my secret, all contentment ends,
And I am lost again.—Oh, do not deem
My thoughts unsanctified!—Yon sacred light,
When first from the Eternal's hand it came,
Before its glows had kindled flames on earth,
Or its bright eye gazed on the sins of man,
Was not more pure than is this sinless heart.
In those lone heavenly wanderings—they were given
A blessing to my spirit, and from Heaven
Alone the blessing came. Ah, doubt me not!

It is communion with my God I hold,
And with his cherish'd Spirits—Should I say
My secret, it was silent—Earth nor Heaven
Would have a voice for me—Look on this ring;
It is the source of this dear happiness.
Should I betray its virtues, thou wouldst gain
Nought; but thy son would lose his all—his soul!
It was a sin, my father; it would draw
The hatred of all nature on my head.
Who would not shrink from that ingratitude
To him who gave the gift, and him who deigns
To serve me with its uses! From the Man,
The holiest of thousands, I received
The wondrous gift; and from his lips I learn'd
Its virtues and its powers—he who died
In pale Marpesus' cave. Now, sire beloved,
Urge thy poor son no farther—not thy hand
Should pluck his only rose.

Andronicus. From Basil's lip,
This I but now was told—he hates thee for
The love which she—forgive me—I will not
Name her unto thee—but, thou know'st the cause,
His hateful jealousy. He hath been here,
Pouring the vials of his wrath upon
My startled head, and threat'ning me with death,
Or punishment to thee.

Leontine. Regard him not;
His wrath is mortal, and will pass away—
A shadow, as himself;— he is a foe
To all of joy or happiness, the which
He hath not soul to share;—he cannot love
That which his mind receives not. Let his wrath

Be to thee as the waves which wave around
The storm-clad Cyclades, yet dare not act
Their fierce, but idle threat'nings. Let it be
The rage of frenzy, which we hasten from,
But mourn it as we fly. The wild bull's wrath,
Which spurneth at the earth, defacing her
With wounds, which her young son, the smiling Spring,
Uplifted on the snowy wings of Time,
Heals with his soft'ning breath—Oh! heed it not
And for the malice of the wondering world—
That cannot harm me, while within my breast
I bear the talisman of peace. Should I
Resign the gift of that same holy man,
Marpesus, sometime hermit, I should be
Once more a ruin, for the Fiend Despair
To stride above in triumph. I should be
The lone—the miserable—the living dead—
The spectre of the past. Oh, sire beloved!
When Mother Earth into her arms received
My Zoe's beauteous form, I did not deem
That even for *thy* peace—that I could live—
Now, I am reconciled; Oh open not
The deep, scarce closed wound! Thou weep'st, ah me,
Melt me not, oh my father, with thy tears!
Thou knowest, to withstand their gentle force
I have no power. I should resign my bliss,
And bow my head, and die.—

Andronicus. O pardon me!
That I have given the pain. Again no more
Will I hold question with thee. Go in peace—
Preserve thy treasure;—mayst thou keep it still
The sun of thy sad day.—

* * *

Scene—The stream near the Marble Cave.—Time— night.

Leontine (alone). Again, again returns the blessed night,
The hour of holiness, and of repose—
To me, of triumph over death and woe:
Let me delay my joy, that I may dwell
On that which doth await me. I am here
Upon the throne of my felicity,
Gazing upon the couch where tranquil lies
Mine own, mine only love, awaiting calm
The signal, and the hour, and the charm
That brings her to my side, the immortal maid,
Beside her mortal lover. Can this be
Transgression! No! Would the Eternal Lord
Permit these visits were they for my harm!—
Yet doth he sometimes punish us by grant
Of that which we do pray for; but the Sage,
Who, in compassion to my anguish, gave
This wondrous ring—and in the sacred stream,
Where the moon kiss'd it, bade me lave the gem
And the encircling gold, had not reveal'd
The secret in the solemn hour of death,
Had it been sinful in the eye of Heaven!—
In that last hour our mortal sense is clear,
And the stern king doth with a steady hand
Unveil the face of Truth, howe'er in life
The form divine was hidden—he had done
With earth and earthly things—and he was then
About to render up a strict account
Of his well-doings; would he then have scal'd
The record with a sin—would he, who was
About to hear the sentence of his fate

From his Almighty Judge, have counsell'd me,
Yea, hurried me to guilt, by raising up
My buried love to my transported eye!
Ah, no!—it is no crime! Ye Elements,
I do attest ye; and Thou, Mightiest Mind,
Soul of those elements, bear witness here,
That I am free of sin! Yea, and their smiles,
The holy stillness of this sacred spot,
And the bright radiance of yon gazing moon,
Do bear my bosom witness—Then once more
To my delightful task—pardon me, air,
And clouds, and water, and celestial fire,
That I do rob ye of a spirit bright,
The fairest in your realms, and give her back
For some short hours solely to the earth,
Of which she is no longer.—Dearest, come!
I am alone, no human breath shall 'file
The air made pure for thee, for I do watch
With zealous care the secret—Come, O come!
In all the beauty of this world, but shrined
In the glory of another. See, I dip
The Ring into the Stream, and I will sing
The song of holiness, to charm thee back
To this earth, and to me:

THE INVOCATION.
When we shall meet
In bowers of bliss;
When we shall greet
With a holy kiss;
When we shall look,
With a soften'd eye,
On the closed book
Of the things gone bye—

When we shall think of this short, dark night,
As the rest that prepares for eternal light,
And look on the bed where they laid us last,
As only the grave of the weary past;
Then shall we smile to think a tear
Should e'er have fallen on a mortal bier!—
But till the beam
Of that holy day
Shall chase the dream
Of hope away:
Till Fate shall burn
With her kindling eye,
This casing urn
Of the spirit high.—
Come from thy couch of holiest dew,
Which the moonbeam shines and sparkles through,
urning each drop to gems, which might—
Circle an angel's brow of light—
To sooth, as heaven hath willed thee,
The anguish of mortality
[A cloud rises from the water and approaches Leontine, then gradually
unfolding, discovers a beautiful female figure reclining in it...]

Leontine. Beautiful spirit of mine only love—
I kiss the spot o'er which thy silver cloud,
Wreathing itself in curls of light, reclines,
And hid thee Sweetest welcome: Oh the joy
To gaze upon thy face, and see thine eye
Beam once again with life! Yet this is death!
Beautiful death! Oh, why do mortals shrink
From thy embrace!—

The Spirit. Because encumber'd with
A load of earth, the spirit scarce can look

Beyond the senses—and that beaming hope
Which is, thou knowest, of immortal birth,
O'ermaster'd is by fear, the earth-born, who,
Is stronger in their bosoms—thou art bless'd
Above mankind, for terror will not stand
By thy departing couch—for thee, the cloud
That hid the grave, is like the ponderous stone,
Roll'd from before its portals—thou hast look'd
Into the dark, and see'st how much to hope,
How little is to fear; but since we met
Thy spirit hath been tortured; greater yet
The trial that awaits thee: when 'tis past
Thou hast no more to fear.

Leontine. So that I lose
Not thee, my sacred love, I am content
To bear all fighter sorrows. I have nought
To tell thee, dear; for in thine absence I
Have only life to bear me silent through
The long and weary day; then I lie down
At eve upon this bank, and watch the sun,
Or wait the rising moon, and mark the stars
Starting from out the heaven, and then I guess
In which of those bright orbs thy beauteous soul
Is wandering; but now I pray thee, love,
Tell me from whence my charm hath summon'd thee?
Where wast thou when the words of power broke
The laws of death's stern empire?

The Spirit. What to thee,
The son of time, was yesternight, I sat
In a huge cloud, which, to its very edge,
Was charged with winds, and tempests. I did wish
To mark its bursting in full majesty

Over the earth, uncheck'd by mortal fears.
So, gathering up mine essence, I reclined
Upon the lightnings flash, and o'er the world
Shot a wild wond'rous light. At first, I deem'd
The meteor flame was harmless, but I found
It was the red bolt of the wrath of God,
And big with desolation: so I left
My throne of vengeance, for I could not bear
To be the instrument of justice, and
Couch'd from its terrors and its glories, in
The fragrant bosom of a half-blown rose.
There, lull'd by music, which the unseen airs
Do bring from the melodious choirs above,
I slept such sleep as holy spirits do
Who are not yet all heaven. When I woke,
I borrow'd from the rose an aerial robe
Of its young delicate hues, and darted far
Upon a golden cloud unto the realms
Of snow and frost eternal—the white point
Most northern of your earth—then I forsook
Mine ether couch, and, for a throne of ice,
Exchanged its melting softness, and it fell
In mist down to the earth. I rested long,
Gazing upon that world, and, when I rose,
I found my mantle had the snowy white
For those to whom th' Omnipotent hath given
His promised boon, the bright and morning
star—
Till then, with me, thou shalt in tranquil joy
Sport in the air, or wing thy flight above
The atmosphere of Earth, the dense, dark robe
Which wraps her wheeling form. The Sun's red beam
By day, shall in a gold garb mantle thee—
At night, the silvery Moon's, and both shall lend

Their rays to be thy chariot. We shall walk
Upon the curved Rainbow, the bright zone
Girdling the universe, and clasping worlds
Within its mighty circle. We shall dart
From orb to orb, and on our brows shall bear
The bright and shooting stars—we shall repose
In worlds of fire, that, nearest to the sun
Revolve their course, and those white orbs which roll
Far distant from his centre—we shall sail
Through seas of ether in our cloudy ship,
And overtake the Morning—we shall list
The song which spirits hear—that song in which
The bands of angels praise the unknown name
Of the Almighty, and whose wondrous sound
Shall even to our accents still remain
Impossible, until the terrible day
Shall make us like to them.—Then, when the Seals
Be open'd, and the Heavens and Earth are doom'd,
Shall the great judgment follow. Nature's things
Shall disobey her laws—Wild Anarchy
And Uproar reign—the shadow of the foot
Of the Eternal shall blot out the Sun.
The Moon be motionless, and faint, and die,
And melt away for anguish—the bright Stars
Fall down with desolation in their light,
And burst asunder, scattering all around
Woe, woe—and bitterness—and there shall be
Blood and not water, and the Angels' hands
Shall grasp the four winds, and then bury them
In their capacious bosoms. Then, all things
Shall groan for air; and, 'midst the pouring forth
The vials of deep wrath, and cries, and shrieks,
And trumpet blasts, and thunderings, and groans
Of Worlds, and shuddering of the crumbled Heaven—

The trampling of the death-steed shall be heard
Bearing his mighty Rider—Summoner
Of mortals, and the Herald of his God—
And then—there shall be silence, in the heaven!–
A pause of death—the uproar shall be still'd—
For the Eternal cometh!—not a sound
Among those myriads to break the awe
Of his tremendous presence—not a sound
Until the Volume of Eternity
Be ope'd—and closed again!—

Leontine. Is it thy voice,
My Zoe, that doth pour these awful tones
Upon my trembling soul?—Oh, how my heart
Shrinks from that day of terrors!—

The Spirit. Fear not thou—
Thou art beloved, and thy spotless life
Hath won high Heaven's grace—thou shalt throw off
This chrysalis case, and rise, and wing thy way
Through fields of peace and light—thou didst but cry
One moment in thy doubts—when my bless'd soul
Ascended from the couch of pain and grief
To liberty, and uncontrolled joy.
I look'd on thee, and though in bliss, there rose
Something, which when on earth, had been a wish
That thou couldst see me, and that I could soothe
Thy grief, and bind thy faith; for thou didst doubt
In thy affliction, and didst fear thyself
Of God and hope forsaken—then the prayer
Of the departing Saint, the holy Man
Of those dim caves, arose unto the Heaven
For thy benighted soul, that thus the faith
Of him whose heart was righteous, should not die

As the guilt-spotted man's—then Heaven
heard—
And when the words of power were said, I swept
Downward from my bright cloud, and with the stream
Mingled my spirit, and from its misty breast,
Rose up before thine eyes.

Leontine. Oh, how my soul
Blesses thy gentle love, that thus survives
The grave, and mingles with eternity
I am more happy in this holy bond,
Than hadst thou lived on earth; and yet there is
One bliss, if it may be, that I would claim—
I hear thee, see thee—might I touch thy hand
With my still earthly lip?

The Spirit. No; for that hand
Were charged for thee with death; and this is not
Thine hour, Oh, Beloved!—but, it comes—
I feel a higher sense of joy than e'er
Mine essence knew before, for soon thou wilt
Unfetter'd be, and thy delighted spirit
Roam blessedly with me; but soft—the air
Is cut before me; something human comes
Tinted with richer hues, for there remain'd,
The roseate colours of my flower-born robe,
Memorial of my visit!—So, when man
Hereafter—as he will—shall seek this spot,
He will behold with wonder the rose hues
Blushing upon the snow!

Leontine. Oh, lot of bliss!
Would that I might partake it!
The Spirit. So thou wilt!

Be faithful to the last, thy lot will be
As is thy Zoe's; not yet perfect, but
Pure as it can be, till th' accounting day,
Which will unbar the golden gates of Heaven,
Shall give us entrance there!

Leontine. But Zoe, say
The sinner when he perishes, how fares
His spirit in its wanderings; doth it dwell
At large, as thine?

The Spirit. No!—for his liberty
Is portion'd to his actions; and that is
As the Almighty dooms him: sometimes he
Sleeps in a torpid sleep—the trance of death—
Dull, heavy, senseless. Such are those who have
Inactive been, and reckless of the gifts
With which they were endow'd; their lives unmark'd
By any good, although unstain'd by crime—
Spendthrifts of time—who dogg'd away their days
As they were nights, or as, instead of time,
Eternity, was written on the brows
Of those who stood around them—The sin-stain'd
Are darker doom'd—sometimes enfetter'd to
The earth which they have quitted, they are bound
To mark the consequences of their guilt,
And watch their issue. The proud Greek of old,
The Macedonian, who with toil and blood,
Strode high above the necks of fellowmen,
And trampled on warm hearts, and wither'd joy,
To raise a mighty empire, was condemn'd—
To see his huge throne shaken, and his friends
Sever, one by one, the columns!—He beheld
The swords his own ambition had unsheath'd,

Plunged in his children's hearts, and saw their shades
Rise trembling from the earth, and mount afar
Above his gloomy dungeon. These are those
Who, chain'd within the womb of the fierce sea,
Are tossed to and fro by the wild storm,
And never rise in air, except to pour
Destruction on the labouring vessel, which
May bear some ancient friend, or child beloved,
Or a lamenting wife. Some are compell'd
To guide the thunderbolt of wrath, which rends
To fragments their own home;—such one I mark'd
Weeping and throwing lightnings, and averting
His eye from where they fell!—And others float
A pestilence in air, and carry death
To the bosoms best belov'd. The Oppressor, who
Rent from the hungry the coarse sordid meal,
To heap up treasures for his heirs, beholds
Those heirs expire of famine, which himself
A deadly blight upon the herb and corn
Breathes o'er the healthy land. The Tyrant's scourge
Is wielded by the Demons, who through space
With stripes pursue the spectre—worse the lot
Of him the envy-struck, who is condemn'd
To watch the bliss of those he most abhors,
And which he strove to crush; he is, indeed,
The tortured—for the penalties of hell
Alone exceed the measure of his pangs.

Leontine. I love the theme, and yet I fear to ask,
Lest with unhallow'd question I offend
The mercy of the Holiest!—If it be
Permitted thee to answer, hath thine eye
Gazed on the Majesty of God?

The Spirit. It is
Permitted thee to question, for thy tongue
Is chain'd from uttering the secrets deep,
Which have been breathed into thy list'ning ear.
Thou art as yet but mortal, but ere long
Thy soul shall be enfranchised; even now
I see, but thou canst not, where near thee stands
The beauteous shadowy king, who looks on thee
With a soft, solemn smile, and whose cold hand
Will fall so lightly on thy youthful brow,
That to the charm'd beholder his still rest
Shall seem like infant's sleep; but guard thee well,
Temptation cometh—danger and distress
Will soon beset thy soul—but be thou firm,
And thou wilt be with me—but not to gaze
Upon the light of the Eternal's eye.
That may not be till after Earth and Heaven
Have pass'd and the great day hath judged
Who merits such high glory; for there is
No higher bliss than that which is reserved.
Draw from the stream the ring—I may not stay
Amid the sons of earth—draw forth the ring,
And give me liberty. Once more alone,
Recall me to thy presence.

Leontine. Psyche, rise!
Soul of my love, ascend yon floating cloud,
Fringing with silver the blue canopy
Of the majestic earth—repose, until
The voice of love recall thee.
I must not
Complain; for murmuring I am too bless'd—
Earth hath some part in me, and I may not,
As yet, disdain her claims. So them, her sons,

I will not chide away.

Enter BASIL, ZENO, and GREEKS, with ANDRONICUS.

Basil. Thou hear'st, he speaks,
Conversing with the demons—now, old man,
Wring from thy son his secret, let him prove
His innocence, or else behold him die!

Andronicus. Insatiate bigot! Oh! my son, my son!
Have mercy on thy father's snowy head;
Bring not the grey hairs to the grave in woe—
Let me not see thy young blood fall to earth,
Ere the old man's hath fail'd—My son, my son!
Let me not lose thee—if thou canst—reveal
Thy secret, and preserve thy life.

Leontine. My life!
It is not worth a crime—I will not break
My promise—but I stand prepared to die.
Weep not, oh father—death for me is bliss.
I go to meet my Zoe—lead ye on.
The punishment of sorcery, though I
Am guiltless of the sin, I am prepared
To meet, oh friends—Peace, dearest father, peace!
We shall soon meet again—Now to the death
My soul, my soul is ready.

Andronicus. Wilt thou, son,
Wilt thou destroy thy father?

Leontine. Wish me not
To live a sinful, and a hopeless man.
Now, if I die, 'tis blessedly—I go.

167

High Heaven will heal thine anguish, as before
It closed the wounds of mine.

Basil. Friends, he will die
Unshrinkingly—see—for himself, he has
No fears. Attack his young heart in its loves—
Seize on his father—let him victim be
Of the young sorcerer's crimes.

Zeno. Old man, thy son
Claims pity for his youth; but thou, whose age
Should have far better taught, and better ruled
His wayward spirit—thou shalt perish, man,
The victim of his secret.

Leontine. Justice! Justice!
What hath my father done?

Zeno. The worst of sins!—
Permitted thy young soul, which, to his charge
The Eternal hath committed, to run wild—
To plunge into unhallow'd mysteries,
Forbidden unto man;–therefore, again,
Thou shalt, as guilty, die.

Andronicus. I am content!

Leontine. Content!—Thou, righteous heaven' hear me! Oh hear!
Sinless is my pursuit, but if ye deem
My wanderings other, why then, let me die;
I stand prepared—bind on these hands your chains,
And let my father go.

Andronicus. I pray ye heed

Nor urge him farther—Ye have wisely judged—
Lead me unto the bed of peace, which waits
To clasp the limbs of the life wearied man.

Zeno. Lead him unto his sentence.

Leontine. I command
Ye stir not. That which from my tortured soul,
With such unhallow'd eagerness ye tear,
Will benefit ye nothing—harden'd hearts
Cannot partake the miracle—This ring—
Oh agony! must I forever lose
My lonely hope—my happiness—and ne'er
Look on her face again: and I must live
This lone and wretched thing. Oh, Zoe—no!
I dare not—will not—Treasured gem, return
Into thy master's bosom.

Basil. Soldiers, bear
The old man to the block.

Leontine. Take—take the ring—
'Tis done—'tis past—I am a wretch—My sire
Clasp me unto thine heart—close—close—thy life
Is sacred—safe—thy son's is—

Zeno. Sorcerer, tell
Thy usage of this ring.

Leontine. I will, but let
Me treasure this last moment of my peace—
I am the wretch doom'd to a violent death,
Who lingers out the last hour of his life,
Unwilling still to part—that ring, it is—

Oh, Zoe, I am mad—my very soul
Is starting through mine eyes—I am all heart,
And that will heave and burst.

Zeno. The ring, the ring—
Sorcerer, declare its powers.

Leontine. It was given
By a most holy man, in my lone hour,
To save me from despair;—he said, that while
I kept the secret, if into this stream,
Beneath the moonbeam, I should plunge the ring,
It would recall to the forgotten earth
The shade of my beloved!

Zeno. Summon her—
I would behold the wonder.

Leontine. For your eyes
Thus envy spotted, in her purity
She will not come to earth—nor is it in
Her power to compass this—the charm was broken
When I reveal'd the secret.

Zeno. Wretch, recall
Her presence to this world, or ev'n now
Thy father dies the death.

Leontine. She said my hour
Was not far distant—can I not escape
These tyrannies, and die!—Oh pardon, God!
I will endure—still—still, I will endure,
And wait till I am summon'd, though it be
In agonies unceasing.

Zeno. I will try
The virtues of thy ring—there, wretch, the stream
Hath swallow'd it forever—silent be
The impious lip of sorcery!

Basil. Music, hark!
And what a gale of sweetness breathes around:
My senses ache; for the oppression grows
Too strong for mortal bearing.

[The Spirit rises in the cloud.]

Leontine. Heaven! She comes,
Mine own, mine only one—She comes once more,
In all her shadowy glory, with a smile
More joyously enchanting—hour of bliss,
I deem'd thee past forever.

The Spirit. Thou hast done
With hours now, beloved. Thy account
With time is closed for ever; now thou step'st
Within the circle of eternity.
Thou hast achiev'd the conquest of thy foe.
The Tempter who beset thee—thou didst give
Thine all for filial love, and wast resign'd
To live a groaning wretch; for this the wreath—
The coronet of Icicles doth wait
To bind thy happy brow, and that thy death
Be favour'd as thy life, lo! I am sent
To summon thee to glory, and to peace—
Now then we part no more—thou art mine own.
Henceforward and forever, the loved charm,
The golden chord is broken. Mourn thou not
Thy father, peace will crown his few short days,

171

For I have open'd his earth-clouded eyes,
And now, with holiest joy, he looks upon us.—
Thou didst once ask to touch my death-chill'd hand—
Approach me now, and on thy lips receive
This holy kiss, and sink upon my breast.—
'Tis done!—Earth take thy part, the silent clay!—
Soul!—to the elements!

Basil. Good Zeno, speak.
Art thou entranced too—what hast thou seen?

Zeno. Nought but a silvery cloud, from which there comes
Sounds as of heavenly music. We have wrong'd
The innocent Leontine!—Is he dead!—
Can that be death!—A smile is on his face!—
O pardon, Heaven, if, in our zeal, we have
Destroy'd the innocent.—Oh, good old man,
Forgive us for thy son.

Andronicus. My son is dead!—
Glory to God!—My heaven-claim'd son is gone.
Gone from all misery—from pain, from sin
Unto eternal bliss.—Glory to God!
The flowers he planted, he hath gather'd young
To bloom in paradise! The stars he lent
To light this earth, he hath reclaimed now
To place within his crown!—Praise be to God!
Glory to the Almighty!

PUBLISHER'S NOTE

This book was produced as part of the Publishing master's degree program at Western Colorado University, Graduate Program in Creative Writing. The students worked cooperatively to produce these fine new editions of worthy public-domain works. The intent is to bring literary classics to a new readership. For the enjoyment of a modern audience, some minor revisions to archaic terms or punctuation may have been made.

Because these works were written in a different time, some attitudes and phrasing may seem outdated to a modern audience. After careful consideration, rather than revising the author's work, we have chosen to preserve the original wording and intent.

ABOUT THE AUTHOR

Mary Diana Dods (1790–1830) was a Scottish author that published a wide variety of works including poetry, dramas, novels, and short stories. Their work appeared in several editions of *Blackwood's Magazine* as well as in other publications such as *The Pledge of Friendship for 1828* and *The Literary Pocket Book* under the pseudonym, David Lyndsay. They also published a collection of fairy tale short stories in *Tales of the Wild and the Wonderful* and a book titled *Dramas of the Ancient World*.

Mary Diana Dods lived under three identities throughout their life. The first was their birth name/identity, Mary Diana Dods. Due to the negative opinions of women authors during this time, they adopted the pseudonym, David Lyndsay. They published the majority of their work under this pen name. In their personal life, they lived under the male identity, Walter Sholto Douglas, a scholar and a diplomat. They were close friends with Mary Shelley and frequently corresponded with her through letters about both writing and their personal lives. They married Isabella Robinson who at that time was pregnant with a child out of wedlock. After Isabella's child was born, Walter Sholto Douglas took on the role of her father. It is still unclear to this day whether they married for love or to protect Isabella and her child from the prejudices they would face.

In their late 30s, they suffered from liver disease as well as other unnamed mental and physical illnesses. This decline in health coincided with their separation from Isabella. After an entire lifetime of financial struggle and debt, Walter Sholto

Douglas was sent to a debtor's prison. While there, they asked a friend to bring them whiskers and a moustache, suggesting that their desire for a male identity extended well beyond the societal benefits of being a man in the 1800s. Walter Sholto Douglas died in debtor's prison around the age of 40 due to medical complications, leaving behind only a legacy and a mystery.

ABOUT THE EDITOR

Anna Stileski is a Publishing student at Western Colorado University where she is becoming well-versed in various aspects of both indie and traditional publishing. She also holds a Bachelor of Arts in Communication Studies with minors in Global Studies and German Language and Literature from Wayne State University.

She is currently the publisher at Bow's Bookshelf, does freelance editing, and teaches English classes as a substitute teacher. Formerly, she worked as a Media Analyst for PRIME Research LP.

Anna's latest project is as an editor of *Gilded Glass: Twisted Myths and Shattered Fairy Tales* (Wordfire Press, July 2022).

WORDFIRE CLASSICS

The Lost World
The Poison Belt
by A. Conan Doyle

The Wolf Leader
by Alexandre Dumas

The Cthulhu Stories of Robert E. Howard
by Robert E. Howard

The Detective Stories of Edgar Allan Poe
by Edgar Allan Poe

The Jewel of Seven Stars (Annotated)
by Bram Stoker

From the Earth to the Moon and Around the Moon
by Jules Verne

The Complete War of the Worlds
The War in the Air
Kipps: The Story of a Simple Man
The Sleeper Awakes and Men Like Gods
by H.G. Wells

Mother of Frankenstein: Maria: or, The Wrongs of Woman &
Memoirs of the Author of A Vindication of the Rights of Woman
by Mary Wollstonecraft

We: The 100th Anniversary Edition
by Yevgeny Zamyatin

One Stormy Night : A Story Challenge That Created the Gothic
Horror Genre
by Lord Byron, Dr. John William Polidori, and Mary Shelley

HOLIDAY CLASSICS
The Ghost of Christmas Always
by Charles Dickens & Kevin J. Anderson

The Santa Claus Stories
by L. Frank Baum

Our list of other WordFire Press authors and titles is always
growing. To find out more and to shop our selection of titles,
visit us at:
wordfirepress.com

facebook.com/WordfireIncWordfirePress
twitter.com/WordFirePress
instagram.com/WordFirePress
bookbub.com/profile/4109784512